The Journey Prize Anthology

Winners of the $10,000 Journey Prize

1989
Holley Rubinsky (of Toronto, Ont. and Kaslo, B.C.)
for "Rapid Transits"

1990
Cynthia Flood (of Vancouver, B.C.)
for "My Father Took a Cake to France"

1991
Yann Martel (of Montreal, Que.)
for "The Facts Behind the Helsinki Roccamatios"

1992
Rozena Maart (of Ottawa, Ont.)
for "No Rosa, No District Six"

1993
Gayla Reid (of Vancouver, B.C.)
for "Sister Doyle's Men"

The Journey Prize Anthology

Short Fiction from the Best of Canada's New Writers

Selected with Douglas Glover

M&S

Canadian Cataloguing in Publication Data

The National Library of Canada has catalogued this publication as follows:

Main entry under title:

The Journey Prize anthology

Annual.

1 –

Subtitle varies.

ISSN 1197-0693

ISBN 0-7710-4429-1 (6)

1. Short stories, Canadian (English).*

2. Canadian fiction (English) – 20th century.*

PS8329.J68   C813'.0108054   C93-039053-9
PR9197.32.J68

Typesetting by M&S
Printed and bound in Canada on acid-free paper

The publishers acknowledge the support of the Canada Council and the Ontario Arts Council for their publishing program.

The support of the Government of Ontario through the Ministry of Culture and Communications is acknowledged.

"Accept My Story" © Robyn Sarah; "Anomie" © Robert Mullen; "Dry" © Jim Reil; "Free Falls" © Vivian Payne; "Landfall" © Joan Skogan; "Long Man the River" © Melissa Hardy; "Notes from Under Water" © Alison Wearing; "Relatives in Florida" © Dorothy Speak; "The Sound He Made" © Richard Cumyn; "Versions" © Genni Gunn; "Water Margins: An Essay on Swimming by My Brother"© Anne Carson. These stories are reprinted by permisssion of the authors.

McClelland & Stewart Inc.
The Canadian Publishers
481 University Avenue
Toronto, Ontario
M5G 2E9

1 2 3 4 5   98 97 96 95 94

About The Journey Prize

The $10,000 Journey Prize is awarded annually to a new and developing writer of distinction. It is made possible by James A. Michener's generous donation of his Canadian royalty earnings from his novel *Journey*, published by McClelland & Stewart Inc. in 1988. The winner of the sixth Journey Prize, to be selected from among the eleven stories in this edition, will be announced in October 1994 in Toronto as part of the International Festival of Authors.

The Journey Prize Anthology comprises a selection from submissions made by literary journals across Canada, and in recognition of the vital role journals play in discovering new writers, McClelland & Stewart makes its own award of $2,000 to the journal that has submitted the winning entry.

This year McClelland & Stewart is pleased to announce the inauguration of another competition. We invited the Ontario College of Art's third-year design class to submit designs for the cover of the anthology, and an award was given to Larry Ioannou, whose design was chosen from among more than twenty entries for this edition.

The anthology has established itself as one of the most prestigious in the country. The Journey Prize is the most significant monetary award given in Canada to a writer at the beginning of his or her career. McClelland & Stewart would like to acknowledge the enthusiastic support of writers, literary journal editors, and the public in the common celebration of the emergence of new voices in Canadian fiction.

Contents

ROBERT MULLEN

Anomie

There was nothing that could roar or run, nothing that could tremble or cry in the air. Flatness and emptiness, only the sea, alone and breathless.
– POPOL VUH

The prisoner, the Indian, the one I have been told is insane, is crouched naked and motionless on the dirt floor of his cell. He hasn't moved, the guard tells me, he hasn't even looked up. Since being brought in two days before he has refused all food and hasn't been seen to urinate or excrete.

"Maybe he doesn't like it here, senhora. Maybe he'd rather be somewhere else. Maybe these walls are in his way and he'd like us to move them."

The door of the cell is opened and then locked again behind me. The prisoner, the pig thief, is slightly built but muscular. His arms and his legs, I notice, standing over him, are still faintly stained with the juice of genipa fruit.

"You've been travelling for a long time," I address him in the pidgin tongue of the river. "You've come a long way. If you won't eat, maybe you'll smoke."

Nothing happens when I crouch beside him or when I take out a cigarette. He seems to be completely at ease, his body

I

relaxed, his breathing slow and deep. He does indeed appear, like certain of the mad, to have removed himself to someplace else entirely.

"That's very well," I say to him. "That's a fine trick. But it will take a much better trick than that to get you out of here, you know."

There is a clue to his behaviour in the weapons which have been taken from him, the roughly hewn bow, the wooden-tipped arrows, and the bark quiver, all of which are of the most primitive possible construction. Before visiting the cell again, I make a trip to the market.

My hunch proves correct. He is no settlement Indian. He'll eat certain of the fruits which I've brought but neither bread nor gruel, whether made from manioc flour or from maize.

He eats without once looking up. He eats slowly, without apparent enjoyment, but he is nevertheless careful to keep turning what he is eating so that no drop of juice should fall and be wasted.

I have brought him a blanket. This, when I place it over his shoulders, he at once shrugs off. I should perhaps, like a mother, have sewn a name into the blanket to prevent its being stolen by the guards.

He still refuses to speak, though I am certain by now that he understands something of what I'm saying to him.

"If he doesn't speak to you today, senhora," the guard grins, "he'll speak to you tomorrow. If there's anything more stubborn than an Indian, it's a woman."

I keep these first visits short. I stay barely long enough to smoke a cigarette, preferring to go away and come back again so that he will get used to the idea that I am someone upon whom he can rely.

His name, I learn on the second day, is Huehue. I consider this good progress. I bring more fruits and plants for him to examine, knowing now that he will allow only those with which he is familiar to remain in the cell.

The guards, amused by me at first, are beginning to find so much coming and going a nuisance.

"They eat grass, senhora. They eat worms. They marry their sisters. What else do you need to know?"

Huehue agrees that he killed a pig. His features tighten. It looked like a pig but it had no hair. His use of the bastard tongue of the river is rough and ready but understandable.

"Tell me," I say. "I wish I could have seen it."

He shakes his head. It was easy. Something wasn't right. The pig didn't even try to run away. He can see now, Huehue says, how this must all have been a trick.

I do some homework with a map. Our pig thief can have come from none of the planting peoples living near the river, as he knows nothing of manioc or maize, of beans or squash. This places him further upstream and further into the jungle, further off in every regard.

He will speak only when we are alone, only when none of the guards are in sight. He learned the pidgin language, he tells me, from his uncle, who made him learn it, who kept pushing thorns into his tongue until he had learned it.

Huehue's dark eyes are following the progress of a spider on the wall.

"He said: If people start telling lies, if they want to kill us, you'll be able to hear that."

He knows tobacco but not cigarettes. He smokes clumsily at first, burning his fingers despite my repeated warnings.

"I didn't know that these had teeth," he shrugs.

Of his own accord he speaks again about the pig. He imitates the animal's grunting and the twang of his bowstring. He shot the pig, he says now, because he was angry, not because he wanted to eat it. He killed the pig because he was ashamed of how it looked.

He has noticed the daily mail plane which passes across the small high window of his cell and he asks me what it is, what it eats, what sort of feathers it has that make it shine so much.

"If a man was here," Huehue tells me, "he would know how to call it."

I expect his memory to be good and it is. This I test by showing him pictures of animals and then asking him to recall them in the order in which they appeared. This task he is able to perform equally well with animals which he has never seen before such as elephants and giraffes.

He asks to keep the pictures afterwards. He wants to look at them again later. He wants to look at them at night, he says, when I'm not there and he's alone.

"Huehue," I remind him, "I'm your friend not your wife."

He shrugs this off. When he hears something that he doesn't like, he makes a motion like brushing away a fly. He wouldn't be afraid at night, he adds then, cagily, if he could have his weapons with him.

My responsibility, it seems clear to me, is not to treat Huehue but merely to assure that he is returned in one piece to that part of the jungle from which he has come. His sentence for the theft of a pig is six weeks, but by paying for the slaughtered animal I manage to have this reduced by two-thirds.

Huehue's weapons, unfortunately, have by this time vanished.

"They were only sticks, senhora. Just wood and feathers. Things like that attract insects."

What I have yet to find out is what could have brought a jungle Indian so far down the river. Huehue claims that this was an accident, that he stepped into a canoe one day without knowing what a canoe was like.

"Huehue," I say, "tell me what was going on just before that."

He turns away. He lacks guile. The change in him is obvious and instantaneous. He says angrily that I talk too much, that I annoy him, that there's no need for me to come there any more.

"Huehue," I tell him, "I'm not a policeman. I'm not a soldier. There was no need for me to come here in the first place."

A launch goes up the river once a week and I arrange for Huehue to be released only just in time for us to walk down to the dock. The less he sees of the town, I'm thinking, the sooner he'll be able to get it out of his mind.

I convince him to put on shorts and a pair of unlaced shoes. In return I bring him some tallow which he uses to grease his short dark hair, leaving it plastered down atop his head afterwards like an upturned bowl.

In the street he walks with his head bowed, not noticing the stares which we are attracting. I have other patients, other commitments, and yet I can't bring myself to send him off on the river alone and unarmed. Already, I notice, he has lost one shoe.

The launch goes up the river only as far as the first rapids and then it turns around. My plan is to accompany Huehue to the rapids and to be back in a week. Once we reach the dock I warn him, I spell this out for him: Only so far and no farther.

He grins at me and on his face is a look I can recall seeing before on the faces of the truly mad.

"Maybe you're afraid that I'll eat you," that look says.

2.

The launch calls at every settlement along the river, at string after string of tumbledown shacks every second one of which, if it isn't a bar, is a whorehouse. What over the years they came here to escape, one can't help observing, those ragged and barefoot men with their canvas sacks of tools, they have in the end merely managed to reproduce.

Huehue's chosen berth is in the bow, in the open air, beside a stack of chicken cages. Having once found this spot, he keeps to it, protecting himself from the heat, from a squall, and from the heavy nighttime dews with a banana leaf.

At night we anchor in the main stream of the river, riding with lanterns swaying fore and aft. These, Huehue remarks, without having bothered actually to examine the lanterns, are large fireflies that someone has tied there.

At the settlements where there is no dock or pier, the pilot merely runs the launch aground and we sit like this, held fast by the mud, until the loading and the unloading have been completed and the inhabitants, whip-thin men with cadaverous faces, wade out to lever us from the mud with tree trunks.

Our fitful progress up the river ends at the foot of a long stretch of rough water where a mission settlement has for some time been situated. From here, I remind Huehue, he will have to make his own way, as I am no sort of person to go traipsing through a jungle.

"You'll come," Huehue shrugs. "I think you will. When you get tired, I'll carry you."

The priest, a Father Joachim, having been alerted by the boat's whistle, is waiting for us on the dock. Father Joachim, a tall man with a white beard, after only the most cursory greeting, demands that Huehue, if he is to come ashore, must first be bound.

"You're a woman," he shakes his head. "You're too kindhearted. You don't know what you've been sheltering."

Only the month before, he tells me, there was a raid. The raid came at dawn and took everyone by surprise because the jungle Indians were known to be shy and normally kept to themselves, appearing on the river for no more than a few weeks each year when various fruit trees were in season. Two mission Indians were killed in the raid and others, including several women, received serious arrow wounds.

"They came without warning. They set fire to huts. They trampled gardens. They sank canoes. It seems that all they came for was to destroy."

I refuse to allow Huehue to be bound, as there is no proof of what part he himself took in the raid, but I agree that he will remain on the launch and away from the compound, where his presence would only stir up trouble.

"Have you had a child of your own?" Father Joachim asks

me. "Can you imagine what it's like to bury someone who was depending on you for protection?"

There is wood to be loaded. The launch will remain until the following morning. In the meantime we tour the many orchards and gardens which surround the mission, each one of which is an experiment, Father Joachim explains, a question posed to which God Himself must answer yes or no.

A marsh has been drained and ditched to produce a rice paddy. A dozen plots have been laid out, divided by low dikes, each plot having been planted with a separate strain.

"So far they refuse to eat rice. They say it looks too much like maggots. The joke is that they still eat those as soon as my back's turned."

Only women are working. The women are wearing shapeless cotton dresses and what appear to be straw coolie hats.

"Those hats were a godsend," says Father Joachim. "A real miracle. As soon as one had a hat, they all had to have one."

Father Joachim, that evening, advises me against going any farther up the river. Whatever obligation Huehue might feel towards me now, Father Joachim warns, will vanish the moment he finds himself back on familiar ground. There is only one rock, only one sure foundation, without which, Father Joachim argues, even the best of men are creatures to their every passing whim.

A boy whose arm was shattered in the raid is brought in and shown to me. The fracture has failed to mend properly and he is to be sent downstream on the launch in the morning to have the arm rebroken.

The boy, whose name is Luis, holds up a useless and crooked limb.

"It was Lizard. I felt him. My eyes were closed, but I wasn't asleep."

Father Joachim smiles but lets this pass. The arm is bad and will have to be rebroken and reset regardless of what crawled over it in the dark to prevent it from healing, Spotted Lizard with his evil ways or a fallen angel.

"It's when they call fireflies the Virgin's lice," says Father Joachim. "That's where I draw the line."

At first light we set out again, this time alone, in a borrowed motorboat which we put into the river above the rapids. Here we find the channel cluttered, strewn with those strange islands which aren't islands at all but merely debris, free-floating rafts of deadfall and rotting vegetation which are the jungle's natural evacuations.

At midday we stop to cut leaves for shade and Huehue takes the opportunity to bathe. I admire and envy the freedom of his nudity, of his maleness, even as I am myself forced to be content with washing my face and arms.

In the evening we go ashore to light a fire and cook, returning to the safety of the boat once we have eaten. Without prompting and without preamble, perhaps because he considers himself already at home, Huehue now describes how a party of raiders, after running all day along secret jungle paths, hide themselves at dusk in hollow trees.

"They wait there. They don't sleep. They just want that night to be over so they can start killing people."

It's the abruptness of this which strikes me. There's no mention of a history, no word of a quarrel or feud, not even the excuse of an enemy.

"They're just waiting," Huehue insists. "They're not saying anything. They're just thinking of what's going to happen when it's light."

We're on the river alone, sitting facing one another over a small bundle of supplies. In the pocket of my skirt is a small pistol which I have carried with me in the past but never used, never fired, never even imagined myself firing.

Huehue asks for a cigarette but doesn't want it lit.

"They know when it's dawn. They know when they see spots of light. Those trees have knotholes."

The raiders leave their hiding places shivering with cold, with excitement, shivering with anger. They're trembling,

Huehue insists, but not because they're afraid. To tremble, perhaps, is not to be responsible.

They start to grunt then. The trembling raiders grind their teeth and tap their bows. The others, the mission Indians inside their compound, hearing this, think that peccaries are rooting in the gardens and come out to drive them off.

The bowstrings snap. The arrows thud. The wounded cry out like children. The blood spurting from the chests of the dying, Huehue says, becomes crimson flowers.

Huehue shakes me awake the following morning in order to complain about having to travel without his weapons. What if we see game? What if we pass someone's camp? If people who don't know us see him without any weapons, Huehue complains, they'll say that a boat with two women in it has just gone past.

Early that afternoon we reach our destination. At Huehue's instruction I guide the boat off the river and into a small stream. Having tied the boat, we then cover it with a layer of leaves to keep out any rain.

"You won't leave today," Huehue predicts. "Otherwise why did we make this roof?"

Not far from the river we come upon a cluster of roughly constructed malocas and not much further up the stream we find a woman and three small children crouched fishing. The woman, whose face and upper body are striped with genipa paint, mumbles something to Huehue in their own tongue.

"She thinks I'm dead," Huehue translates. "She says a dead person's brought me back."

Huehue too steps into the stream. He touches the woman and each of the children lightly on the head and then he too commences fishing, using a stick to stir up the dead matter lying on the bottom and then snatching out with his free hand whatever tiny creatures this disturbs.

Smoke is seeping from the roof of his maloca when we return. Two more adults and an older child are squatting inside, all three holding their hands up in front of their black-striped faces in order to peer at me from between their fingers. A monkey has been killed and is already roasting over the fire. The minnows we have brought back are threaded onto wooden skewers to be cooked, the still struggling crayfish merely dropped onto the coals.

The other man in the hut is Yano, Huehue's uncle. He too speaks pidgin, Yano informs me. He is also the oldest and it is to him that I must speak from now on, he announces, in order to prevent what I say from being misunderstood.

Huehue's response to this is mumbled under his breath. This is the teacher who pierces his pupil's tongue with thorns. This is not a man with whom one argues.

The monkey, black with its own singed hair, is removed from the fire and broken at the chest into two portions. The limbs are torn off and distributed. The skull ends up in the hands of the children, who sit over it silent and grim faced, patiently spooning out its contents with twigs.

After the meal, I lie down without undressing on a mat woven from rushes. Birdcalls awaken me, creaking branches, other sounds which I can't identify. Awakening for the last time at dawn, I discover three small bodies curled against my legs.

The fire is stirred. Some old bones are found and reheated. Yano tells me then to go outside to the stream and to wash my face because visitors will soon be arriving.

"Do you understand?" Yano says. "Do whatever you have to. Later on people will be watching you."

Rather than sit and allow myself to be inspected, I turn the day's ceaseless visiting into a clinic. I peer into eyes and ears, manipulate limbs, press stomachs, listen to the beatings of their hearts, in this way hoping to eliminate disease as an explanation for the raid or Huehue's "accident."

By the end of the day I have found nothing more than the usual teeming parasites of the region.

"Well," says Yano, "we don't know why you did that. We don't know what you've taken."

In the evening, it's the children's turn. I'm made to kneel and one examines my eyes, one prescribes muddy water, one acts out the way in which I held open people's mouths with a stick while I looked down their throats.

Yano, when he has had enough of the children's noise, stops the game by threatening them with a brand from the fire.

"Children are a mistake we made," Yano frowns. "We should have killed them as soon as they appeared."

I watch and I listen. Something is wrong here, but what? Yano too is short and muscular, but with a protruding belly. The children are huddled now, giggling, beneath a piece of hide.

"We were on a path. We could see where we were going. We thought: Let those children come if they want to because they'll be able to follow us."

That's all. The subject is dropped. Yano asks for a cigarette which he breaks open and crumbles up in his palm, afterwards tamping both the tobacco and the paper into a small cane pipe.

He asks me then if we came up the river in a boat moved by the sun. In the morning, Huehue has told them, the sun blew on the boat, making it smoke, and in the evening the sun pulled the boat along behind it on a rope made out of vines.

"I would have liked to see that," Yano sighs.

3.

I have been able to count twenty malocas in the area, some holding as many as a dozen people. These structures are built in a day and are used for only a single season, only for as long as it takes to harvest the fruit as it ripens and to hunt down whatever game the fruit trees may have attracted. Then, it seems, the groups scatter, fanning out in their small family bands into the jungle.

"We see someone's tracks," Huehue tells me. "We see someone's campsite. We say: If they're here already, we'll go somewhere else."

This isn't a complaint, this is their manner of being. Coming together when food is abundant and spreading out again as it becomes scarce is a strategy imposed by the world in which they live.

"But then something changed," I suggest to Huehue. "I'm wondering what that was."

Huehue glances over to the mats to see whether Yano is listening. Then, ignoring my suggestion, he begins speaking again of the canoe, of how it got away from him and left him looking at nothing but water.

"We said: What are these? Why are they so big? These must be the bowls that those people eat from."

We hear shouting from the direction of the river. A snake has been discovered. A boa constrictor has been found in the shallows where the men go to bathe. The news is passed from maloca to maloca by means of shrill whistles.

By the time we reach the river, the snake has already been killed, its head having been smashed into a bloody pulp with stones.

"He wanted to eat us," Huehue grins. "Now we're the ones who'll have a meal."

Lianas are cut and tied around the body of the snake. While some pull on these lines to drag the creature from the river, others work with poles to lever it from the sucking mud. Eventually a line is passed up and over the branch of a tree and the carcass is by this means hauled up and left to dangle in mid-air.

I join the women, who are already picking up firewood. The women have remained calm, not sharing in the excitement of the men or the children, who, egged on by the men, are pelting the snake with stones and clumps of dirt.

The butchering commences at the tail. Two men cut and two more operate the rope, lowering the carcass as necessary in order to bring more of the creature's pale stringy flesh within reach of the jagged pieces of tin which the butchers employ as knives.

The meat is roasted in long strips, over numerous small fires. Each strip, once cooked, is handed first to a man, who bites off a portion of it for himself and then passes on the rest to a woman or child. Within an hour of the snake's having been discovered, all that remains of it is a heap of bones and vertebrae.

Afterwards, when we're resting, Yano suddenly stands up, spits out the chewing stick with which he has been cleaning his teeth, and demands to know why I have come there.

"Was it to see the Old Men? Was it that? Why not tell us now? Was it to see the Grandfathers or for something else?"

I am no hunter but I can imagine that moment during a hunt when the hunter first senses something, when he first catches a glimpse of fur or feathers through the leaves, a moment that sets his heart racing.

"Are they here?" I say. "I wasn't sure. If they're here, I'd like to see them."

Yano begins to pace back and forth, punching at the sky with his fist as he speaks. He thought so. He thought that was why. Why else would I have followed Huehue all this way when we don't even copulate?

The three of us are to go, stopping off at the maloca on the way so that the men can pick up their weapons.

"We'll show you their houses," Yano says. "You can see for yourself. Don't blame us if those houses are empty."

From the maloca we plunge straight into the jungle, following no path that I can discern but keeping to the drier and clearer ground, skirting where necessary patches of deadfall and thickets of bamboo and thorn trees. We follow no path and, by staying on dry ground, we leave none.

Yano, who is leading, stops now and then to sniff the air and to peer up into the closely woven tapestry of leaves and vines which forms the jungle's roof.

"Are they there?" Huehue whispers. "If they're there, why aren't they pissing?"

This is how they find monkeys. Monkeys can be identified not only by the shells and husks which they drop but also by the strong and distinctive odour of their urine.

The farther into the jungle we go, the farther we move from

thc rivcr, thc tallcr thc trees and the higher the canopy. Looking up now, I find, can be as dizzying as peering over the edge of a precipice.

Our circuitous walk through the blue-lit jungle brings us at last to a great outcropping of sandstone. This cliff rises a hundred feet or more, breaking through the canopy and so admitting here a purer and more dazzling light.

The face of the cliff, I can begin to see, is pockmarked with shallow holes.

"This is where they live," says Yano. "They made these houses. We don't know why they've changed their minds."

We stand side by side shading our eyes. The cliff is stained with dung. The holes are clearly nests. The Old Men, the Grandfathers are – or were – a colony of birds, drawn, like the Indians themselves no doubt, by the yearly abundance of fruit.

Once, twice, three times now, says Yano, there has been nothing in the nests.

"Maybe we're lying. Maybe we made this up. If you see something, tell us."

The holes are empty. The cliff is deserted. Whatever nested here in the past has not returned.

"Yano," I say. "I can see what you see. No more and no less."

Huehue leads the way back through the jungle, Yano having complained that he feels tired. This strange fatigue grows worse as we walk, causing the two of us to fall further and further behind until Huehue is no longer in sight.

Then Yano suddenly stops and turns to face me, places both hands on my breasts, and pushes me back against the trunk of a tree.

"You need a child in you!" he hisses.

Perhaps, it has crossed my mind, but not his.

"Where is it?" Yano growls. "Where have you hidden it?"

The layers of clothing blunt his initial thrust. Using my greater weight I then force him to retreat, shoving him backwards, walking with him still clutching at my buttocks until he loses his balance.

He turns away. He breaks off a branch to use as a walking stick and picks up his bow.

"So this is how you are," he shrugs.

The birds, the Old Men, are green parrots. Huehue shows me a green feather, turning it in the light of the fire to show off its brilliance. Yano is sitting silently on his mat plaiting an armband out of monkey hair.

This is what first started people listening to the parrots, Huehue says, the way that their feathers are shining. This is what starts people following the birds when they see them moving through the jungle.

"We say: Be like them. Do the same. Try to keep up. Don't we want our lives to shine?"

Seldom in their lonely wanderings through the jungle will they see the sky or stars. What better guide, what better calendar under these circumstances than the seasonal flights of a particularly visible bird?

"Men do this," Huehue adds. "Women follow the men."

I don't know why the nests are empty. I do know that once a bird starts to become scarce it also becomes valuable, it becomes an irresistible temptation, and any settler, any prospector, any rubber or chicle gatherer who spots that bird on the river will immediately drop everything in order to pursue it.

4.

The women are up early to complete their preparation of a wild wine. For this they have mashed and chewed up spoiled fruit, employing for their vessels a number of holes in the ground which they have lined with pebbles. Now they must keep stirring the foaming juice and watch over the holes to keep away insects.

The women have thought up a name for me, Huehue says. The women have started calling me Whitehair, this although my hair is by no means white or even blond but merely a somewhat lighter colour than their own.

We begin drinking the mildly fermented fruit juice before

midday. We drink near the holes, squatting, using for bowls the hard outer casings of certain nuts.

"At first nothing happens," Huehue grins. "This is how we are. We piss it all away."

Were it not for the novelty of this wine, I would have already been on the river, already on my way back to the mission. Yano's behaviour of the day before, while easily enough dealt with at the time, turns out to have frightened me far more than I at first allowed myself to admit.

"We say: This is nothing. This is water. Those women couldn't make a tick drunk."

Huehue asks for a cigarette. This alerts me because I have noticed that he never asks for anything unless he intends to give back something in return. He has decided to tell me, Huehue says, about the log races.

"We're hunting, do you understand. We're killing things. Then we start to hear those Old Men."

I myself would hear nothing. The Grandfathers don't speak pidgin. All that I would hear would be a lot of squawking.

"We say: We'd better stop now. We'd better do something else. We'd better go and make those logs."

This is the first thing they do when they reach the river. The logs are cut and stripped of their bark. The logs are painted. The men decorate the logs with feathers and then they run through the jungle carrying the logs on their shoulders.

"We're running, we're running, we're getting tired. We say: This is good. This is what they told us. A little further."

This is the sex act surely. This is simulation. This is magical increase. While the women and children build malocas and look for firewood, the men play sacred games.

The men go in one group down to the river to bathe and to put on fresh genipa paint. The women, who can't leave the wine sinks unattended, slip away a few at a time up the stream, returning with their hair bejewelled with lemon-scented flowers.

More green feathers appear, this time set into headdresses and armbands. Huehue alone possesses more than a dozen of these, six of which he obtained from one of his grandfathers, he claims, and eight from the other, who was fatter.

We set out all together for the cliff this time, men, women, and children, picking up sticks and branches as we walk. A grandfather is a green parrot, a green parrot is a grandfather: In what way, such propositions may be inviting us to reflect, are they the same?

Coming out at the cliff face, stepping from the semi-darkness of the forest into that flood of yellow light, this time makes my head spin. The light, the open sky, the single wall with its empty niches, brings to my mind this time the image of a bombed cathedral.

Fires are lit at the foot of the cliff, one each for each of the hunting bands, one fire for each maloca. There is no meat because neither Huehue nor Yano has hunted, but the women have found some breadfruit and one of the children has captured a tortoise on the way which he forces into the fire with a stick.

The drinking hasn't slowed. Small amber pools lie fermenting all around us in natural basins among the rocks. Those who can no longer walk to these pools nevertheless continue shouting out for more.

Yano too has been drinking since early in the day but his eyes and his speech are still clear.

"We told the women. We said: Stop being so greedy. Stop making so many new people."

This is Yano's story but even in this version of events the women are no pushovers. The women say no. They won't. A pot isn't at fault, the women argue, for what someone puts into it.

"We should kill them, we say. We should make them sorry. A broken pot doesn't have to hold anything."

The women, however, have an answer for this as well. The women aren't even frightened.

"Who'll bring water?" the women say. "Who'll pick up wood? Who'll blow on the ashes when men get cold?"

The breadfruit is raked from the fire and discovered to be rotten. Rather than a calamity, however, this is seen as a good joke. The joke is that while the food that we intended to eat is spoiled, it has nevertheless provided us with a snack of small grey worms.

The women, when they want to urinate, go off in twos and threes into the trees. The men merely stand up and turn their backs. Huehue, while he is on his feet, takes the opportunity to point out various people at another fire who he now claims are responsible for the raid on the mission.

Huehue squats down again and picks up his bowl.

"They were already here. They were hiding. They say that they heard something."

Impatient, hungry, unable to wait any longer, one of the bands arrived back before the others and picked a number of trees clean of fruit, picking fruit that hadn't even ripened yet, Huehue claims, just so that no one else could have it.

Huehue produces a cigarette that he's been saving and lights it from the fire.

"What did they hear? Who told them that, a crow?"

Yano, pot-bellied Yano, tells another story. The first time anyone came to the cliff, says Yano, they come to look for insects. They come without paint, without feathers. They come to turn over the rocks.

From their houses on the cliff, the Old Men notice this.

"Look how skinny they are," the Old Men say. "Why were they even born?"

The Old Men are green parrots. The Old Men have chosen this bird because of its feathers. No other bird keeps its feathers as shiny and free of lice. The Old Men decide to help human beings because they're so disgusting.

No one sees the wind when it comes and no one sees those birds when they swoop down and pick up a child.

"This will seem strange at first," the Old Men tell it. "But later on, you'll see why."

The Old Men bring the child food. When the nest is fouled, the Old Men clean it. Whenever the newcomer remembers its former parents and starts to cry, one of the birds puts his penis into the boy's mouth and ejaculates.

This is how it gets started. This is how they got those birds for grandfathers, Yano concludes. This, stripped of its casuistry, is yet one more episode in malekind's enduring fantasy of engendering itself.

It's dark and the fires are burning down. From the darkness, I can hear the sound of retching.

"Huehue," I say, "I'm thinking of your feathers. I'm wondering how you got them."

I'm thinking of the empty nests. I'm thinking that there is an occasional misfortune of which one is purely the victim but many more at which one oneself can be shown to have connived.

For feathers, Huehue says, a man must first fast for many days.

"He has to be thin. He has to hope nothing sees him."

He goes after fasting to a place where he knows that there are parrots and he builds a blind, setting out a piece of fruit as bait. He crouches in the blind, hiding, until one of the birds comes down for the bait and then he grabs it, he pulls it through the wall of the blind, and he strangles it.

"He talks to it. He tells it why he did that. Afterwards it gives him its feathers."

5.

I must sleep more deeply than I intend because when I open my eyes it's morning and all of the fires but our own are deserted. We're the last, Yano immediately starts complaining. About the last, people say: Here come the buttocks.

Yano rouses the other women and sends them to search

through the ashes of the abandoned fires for food. A few charred bones are found which, when broken open, yield a little marrow.

The women, Huehue tells me now, think that I should travel with them. They say that they'll walk slowly for the first few days until I learn to keep up. They like not knowing where to find their children in the mornings, the women say, and then seeing them all come crawling out of my clothing.

We move back through the jungle to the maloca. Here the women at once begin gathering up their belongings, rolling up gourd pots, gourd ladles, and various bits of wood and clam-shell into the woven mats on which they sleep.

I'm thinking that it's over, that there's no more to be said, that I should go and try the motor of the boat, but instead I stand watching, with my hands in the pockets of my skirt, until all of them except Huehue have set off.

Huehue then tells me to follow him. When I don't move at once, he tugs at my sleeve, insisting, anxious as a child that I should be a witness to one last trick.

Not far from the maloca we find the logs, the painted logs used in log races strewn haphazardly on the jungle floor.

"No one's left here," Huehue grins. "No one will know this."

Picking up a stone, he begins pounding on the first of the logs. A few substantial blows and the log splits in half. The racing log, a palm trunk, is already rotting, and rotting palm wood yields grubs.

These, along with some termites, Huehue carefully removes and folds into a leaf along with a little of the wood pulp.

"Keep on eating," Huehue tells the grubs. "Get as fat as you can. Later on someone else will do the same."

One can continue to function in the end without one's gods. One comes to learn this. One learns this long before one learns how to admit it.

Huehue, having ransacked all the logs, folds up the smaller packages into a large one, securing it with a length of creeper.

"Maybe you think we'll forget you," he says. "Maybe that's why you've stopped talking."

He says that they won't. He says that they've made up a story to help them remember, a story about how white women once had no vaginas.

No one knows how this happened but the Old Men agree to fix it.

"That's how they are. They're always helping people."

The Old Men, the Grandfathers, the green parrots, fly over the white women dropping pebbles, dropping pebbles on them, opening up vaginas in the tops of the women's heads, and it's because they want to keep these vaginas a secret, Huehue says, that white women always wear hats.

This is the way that it finishes, with the gift of a story. We shake hands. We understand each other. We like one another, I think. The undergrowth parts and then it closes again and Huehue's quiet footfalls all too soon give way to the timeless droning of cicadas.

GENNI GUNN

Versions

W hen I was two, my sister Marcia who was three and a half, lifted me up over a balcony railing and held me upside down by the ankles suspended two storeys above the street. When my mother walked into the room and saw this, she slipped off her shoes, took a deep breath and held it, then slowly crossed to the balcony so as not to startle Marcia.

Depending on my mother's mood, this part of the story is more or less elaborate. Sometimes she is wearing high heels (blue, to match her dress); other times Chinese red brocade slippers (and doesn't take them off); sometimes she is wearing black laced boots which would take too long to remove, so she has to walk on tiptoe very very slowly and carefully. The distance varies too: eight steps, fifteen, twenty-five. Sometimes, and this when she's feeling particularly dramatic, she is coming home from a friend's or the train station, and sees me from below. Then she must climb the stairs (often she can't find her key immediately and doesn't want to ring the bell in case Marcia is distracted).

The story always ends with my mother grabbing my ankles the exact moment Marcia lets go of them. And then, my mother leans back and says, "The trouble with Marcia is that she was so jealous," implying that Marcia's entire life has been one enormous mistake (this being the first) made up of escalating small ones. A little like a novel, perhaps, though Marcia doesn't think of it in these terms.

When Marcia tells this story, it is almost identical but for two things: the intent and the ending. She says there was a parade that day moving below the window and I was too small to see over the balcony. I cried, waving my arms in the air. Marcia was watching the multi-coloured floats of tissue-paper flowers while hopping wildly from foot to foot to the rhythm of marching bands. She pointed and pointed but I was just too small. Then she had an idea (sometimes, she attributes this idea to one of the passing floats – the three bears sitting on small chairs or the elephant perched on its hind legs on a box). She went inside, dragged the piano stool to the balcony and lifted me onto it. Then she stood on it herself, and carefully hauled me over the railing. Here, the versions coincide, although Marcia always stresses the fact that she never let go of my ankles, in fact, was annoyed at my aunt for pulling me back before I could see the giant blue float with the yellow ducks on it. She's certain it was my aunt, and not my mother, of whom she has no recollection until years later. She always ends the story with, "The trouble with Mother is that she keeps trying to fit herself into other people's pasts," like a new character who shows up in a rewrite but who nobody recognizes.

When my aunt tells me the story, she is lying on her bed in Italy, in a darkened room, shutters tight against the August heat, and I am reclined on a pink chaise lounge smoking Canadian cigarettes. She recalls the minutest details which imply that her story is the real one, or perhaps that she has the best imagination. For example, she says it was the 13th of August and she was wearing her black dress with the tiny blue flowers and the V-neck. We had all returned recently from our weekly visit to the cemetery where Marcia had thrown a tantrum when she wasn't allowed to pull all the petals off all the flowers. (My aunt had been widowed two years, she tells me.) In order to appease Marcia who was still crying, she took us upstairs to the balcony to watch the parade. After twenty minutes or so, she carried out the piano stool because her arms were aching from holding me up to the railing. She says Marcia was restless, thirsty; she had thrown her hat into the street and was now wailing and pointing at it as it wafted down.

My aunt gets up and goes to the kitchen, while I light another cigarette and push butts to one side of the ashtray. She returns with two glasses of orange juice and soda and lies back down on the bed. I have not seen her for twenty years and am anxious for her to fill the spaces in my memory, to confirm or deny, although why I should believe her versions, I don't know.

She says she only left the balcony for a few moments. She doesn't place blame or justify her actions, although she does tell me it was not easy looking after two little girls at her age.

The rest of the story coincides with Marcia's and this relieves me because two people surely couldn't invent the same details.

I don't recall the incident, although through hearing it, I've memorized the balcony and my position on it. I even imagine I can recall the people on the street at the time, although here logic fails me and when I retell this story, it is many years later and the balcony is on the 28th floor of a Vancouver apartment building. I am there with Harris, or Andrew, or some other English name. He is my lover of some weeks and it is his birthday. This story always occurs at night, downtown, when I can imagine the Vancouver skyline and the ships anchored in the harbour.

In the story, we've had a fabulous dinner – steak and lobster (flown in from the East Coast) – then Harris has blindfolded me (black silk scarf – implying ritual) to prepare me for a surprise. He leads me to the balcony door and slides it open. I feel the warm summer air and hear tires on wet pavement below although it is August and it hasn't rained for thirty-six days. Harris urges me over the sill onto the balcony, and walks behind me, his arms around my waist until a certain moment when he tells me to stop. Here, the details vary, according to my mood. Sometimes only his fingers touch my waist; other times I am leaning back against him and laughing. Either he removes the blindfold or I reach back and undo the knot. The moment I can see, however, the versions merge.

Harris has removed the balcony railing, and I am balanced precariously at the edge.

How long I stand there depends on the reaction of my audience. Then, Harris slowly pulls me back to the safety of the sliding glass door which feels solid even though I can see through it. I try to end the story here, by saying, "The trouble with me is that I'm too trusting," thereby absolving Marcia of all guilt, although she doesn't appear in this story.

More often than not, however, I am pestered into giving a denouement, when we all know some stories are best left at the climax. I vary these too. Sometimes I run out of the apartment forgetting my shoes and car keys and have to buzz Harris and go back up and retrieve them; other times I slap him across the face, square my shoulders and leave in a most dignified manner; other times I push him hard and he lands with his head over the edge of the abyss and begs for mercy. With this ending, I say, "The trouble with Harris is that he underestimated me," when actually it wasn't Harris at all, but my mother who keeps pushing me to the edge by restructuring my past until I'm unbalanced and can't trust my own memories.

When my father tells this story, he sets it in London, England (where he was at the time), on a foggy, grey day (probably to reconcile setting and content). He has just finished the first page of a letter to my aunt (my mother is with him), when he hears the cry of a child outside his window. He throws open the balcony doors in time to see a small girl holding a baby by its ankles over the railing of a balcony above. The girl is crying, "I can't hold her any more," and the baby is shrieking. Here, my father says he distinctly recognized those voices as Marcia's and mine (even though he hadn't seen either of us since I was born). My father climbs the outside of his balcony railing, secures his feet into the rod ironwork and holds out his arms. Sometimes the balcony is concrete and he straddles it and has to lean into the street; other times it is wooden and rickety and he has to balance carefully to keep it from toppling. Often he is fully dressed because he is expecting an important visitor; occasionally he has just come out of the shower and is wearing only a towel.

Below, a circle of people hold up the edges of a blanket or some-times, the street is deserted. The ending, however, is always the same: the girl drops the baby which my father catches without incident. He ends this story with, "The trouble with children is that they have no concept of danger," which is true, considering how Marcia and I keep perching on the edge of a balcony, watching memories which shift dangerously from narrator to narrator and before I know it, I can't tell fact from fiction any more, and this is really dangerous because it implies that my life, the one I am trying to live so accurately, can and will be distorted, reordered, adjusted, and will emerge, years later, as a piece of fiction in some stranger's living room.

Now photographs. Yes, they tell a more precise story. Here's a family classic. In the middle of evergreens is a large tree with a thick branch on which my mother, Marcia and I are all stand-ing. We are smiling, and wearing identical puffy dresses in pastels, with frilly crinolines underneath. My mother's mouth is especially beautiful; the crimson lipstick accentuates the whiteness of her teeth. Each of us is hugging the tree trunk or each other with one arm, and waving with the other to my father who is taking the picture. You have to look close to see that Marcia is wearing track shoes and she is standing on one of my mother's bare feet.

JOAN SKOGAN

Landfall

The second officer had drifted safely past more than half of the *Aleksei Chirikov*'s winter fishing voyage on the Bering and Okhotsk Seas before he enmeshed himself in memory and dreams. Days, he had worked his bridge watches along with a shift in the processing factory below-decks when the catch was heavy. Nights, he had drunk tea with the third officer, or sat in the messroom to watch 16 mm. film in which soldiers or gypsies or Cossacks streamed across an empty plain, their silhouettes dark against the sky as they sang a sombre, defiant chorus into the distance. He had kept up his paperwork. He had slept.

In his bunk, wool blankets weighted the length of his body, filling his nose and mouth with their cold, animal odour. A white cotton pillowcase transmitted the slight dampness of its enclosed feathers to his cheek until he turned and crossed his arms over his chest to lie, unmoving, in the first shallow layer of sleep. Later, he would curve himself onto his right side, always the starboard side to steer away from nightmares at sea.

He allowed only itinerant, easily ignored characters to cross the geography of his dreams during the first half of the voyage: the eight-year-old boy he used to be in the high-ceilinged flat in the south; Konstantin from next door at the same age, shivering in an unravelling sweater, one of his eyes bright with mischief, the other dark with foreboding: Vitus Bering, his voice mixed into the splash of snowmelt in the Anadyr River, supposed to be saying how to get upstream to the source, but he's talking some unintelligible foreign tongue only explorers understand.

After nearly three months at sea, the second officer weakened and let down the barrier at the border of his dreams, exhausted, perhaps, by the stubborn southeast gale which had been shunting the ship around the Shelkov Gulf for days. Asleep on the long swell the winds had left behind, he saw himself, not the solemn-faced, soon-forgotten child of earlier nights, but the same man he was then, standing again in a room full of spilled wine and shouting in the port of Petropavlovsk. A woman leaned over a corner table, whispering words he couldn't hear, any more than he had heard them when he sat across from her in the flesh, cinnamon-and-sweat-scented, the night before the *Aleksei Chirikov* sailed.

The second officer opened his eyes and wedged the bulk of his top blanket behind his back to hold his body still as the ship rolled down one side, hesitated, returned upright for an instant, then rolled again. Pushing his feet against the bottom of the bunk to stretch the muscles that knotted his legs almost every night at sea, he wondered why he had wanted to escape the woman in the bar when he had nothing to do, once he was standing in the muddy street outside the place, but lurch toward the pier where the *Aleksei Chirikov* lay waiting for him. He did not understand how he had been able to recreate the Petropavlovsk woman from memory so easily, even if she was only a dream, when most mornings, as he rose and braced himself against the tin locker to keep his balance, he could not, for the first moment or two, remember the *Aleksei Chirikov*'s name, or call sign, or even which ocean they were fishing.

The tin locker's shabby, unchanging presence was a comfort to him, as well as a reminder of where he was. Over the course of the voyage, he had come to know his cabin better than he had ever known the rooms he shared with his wife when he was still married. Those rooms had sometimes seemed as if they should belong to another man, someone whose fingers did not catch in the web of his wife's crocheted shawl, tearing the strands and making her cry; a man who smiled more, who knew without being told that when he returned from the ship, his wife wanted him to dance with her beside their bed before they got into it.

The cabin's furnishings had become members of the second officer's family, whether they were new and unspoiled, like the small mirror Sasha, the deck bo's'n, had supplied to him, or worn with use, as was the tin locker, whose gaping door required constant contrivance with tape and cord to keep it from banging relentlessly. There was a hook that reminded him – he couldn't say why – of one of his girl cousins each time it loosened itself on a fifteen degree port roll to chime a pure belled note against the steel door frame. His armchair required him to lean to the right and slightly forward to accommodate his body to its crooked frame. When he had finished his bridge watch each day, he sat in this chair at the plywood table bolted to the bulkhead.

The table and the shelf above it held icons of the unimaginably distant earth, remembrances of vanished kitchens and garden plots, things the second officer always intended to eat or drink or admire, but more often forgot until they rotted or spilled or rolled off the table: soft, pink-cheeked apples and hard-boiled eggs with grey, finger-smudged shells, given him by Raisa, the ship's bufetchitsa; hard toffees and lemon drops wrapped in purple and white paper printed with dancing horses which always stuck to the candy; a packet of black tea leaning against a glassful of coarse-grained sugar crystals; a cracked, flowered cup; a bundle of birch twigs, the jagged-edged leaves gone brittle and dull, but still green.

The plywood table was intended for the paperwork connected to the second officer's additional duties as provisions officer and assistant supercargo. If the pale northern sun pushed through the morning sky, he might see the shadow of a petrel or some other seabird fly across his papers before he went up to the bridge. A ribbon of light refracted from the waves below could dance over the cargo logs and up the bulkhead. He worked at the table when he had finished his watch on the bridge and was not needed in the factory during the late afternoon and on into the evening, comforted by the yellow gleam of his desklight in the early dark as he sorted food lists and cargo hold plans and tallied the numbers of cartons filled with frozen headed and gutted or filleted pollock.

He stopped writing now and then to stare through the salt-smeared glass beside him at the darkening sea, then glance at the picture pinned above his table. This picture, torn from an old issue of *Novy Mir*, showed a dusty white road, a path, really, winding through green countryside. The curves of the road were entirely human and full of promise, he thought each time he looked at them, in a way the sea never was.

Life is not a walk across a field. In the fourth month of the voyage, the second officer looked up at the picture of the white road and remembered his father's mother reciting the field proverb at every calamity from a cracked egg to the death of her daughter-in-law. The old woman had slept on a couch with him when he was small and his mother was still alive, when they lived in the Crimea. His grandmother sighed often in her sleep, terrifying him muttering about famine bread, the dense, bitter loaves made from grass she had eaten when the grain was gone, years before he was born. She woke him once in the middle of the night, he remembered, to tell him she had dreamed she saw Lev Tolstoi on the boardwalk in Sevastopol. She was afraid of him, she said. He looked furiously angry and as if he had no legs. It had all truly happened, she insisted, once upon a time when she was a girl, on the boardwalk in Sevastopol by the Black Sea.

Tolstoi must have been sitting in a wheeled wicker basket chair, the second officer thought when he awoke before dawn the next morning, if it had been him at all. He cared nothing for Tolstoi. Chekhov, maybe. There was some value to him. He had visited the ports and prisons on Sakhalin, for one thing, and, according to his wife, he had uttered an incomprehensible question about sailors as he lay dying. The second officer felt he would have been able to tell Anton Chekhov what he wanted to know about sailors if he had been at his bedside. I know my work, he thought. I know the Bering Sea and the Barents, the north Pacific and the Okhotsk Sea. Awake and asleep, I remember the land, even if I no longer know what to do with it, or it with me, when I am on shore. That is all there is to being a sailor.

Weariness washed over the second officer. He smoothed the bedclothes and lay back in his bunk, but sleep was gone from him. He opened his eyes and saw the shapes of the armchair and the tin locker, huge and strange in the dark. He got up to unlatch his porthole, put out his hand to feel the river of wind and rain flowing past *Aleksei Chirikov*. He touched his cool, wet palm to his cheek and his tiredness retreated a little. There was a street in Moscow called Sailors' Rest, he had heard, although he had never been able to find it on his hurried visits to the city. Now, standing beside the porthole open to the night, he wondered if Sailors' Rest Street were well-lighted or dark, if people walked along it cheerfully crowded together, calling out to one another and smiling at known faces, or if they went alone, their shoulders hunched over bags and bundles, their eyes avoiding one another's glances.

These imagined scenes slid away from the second officer, and in their place came a memory of a foreign street where he had stood, suspended in the night for a moment, on his way back to the ship. He could not remember which ship. Not the *Aleksei Chirikov*. The side of the street he had walked along lay on the edge of a small park, facing a line of stores whose clouded front windows were shuttered with cardboard for the night. A man's running shoe, blue and white, thick-soled, lay on its side, close to his feet when he stopped. Its mate waited on the grass beside the pavement. He heard the soft, repeated thud of a basketball bouncing from backboard to concrete within the park, although the player was hidden by the complicated and delicate structure of some wooden bleachers.

He recalled the huge, broad-leafed maple trees glowing copper under the street lights beside the park, and how he had, for that moment, seemed to be in the right place at the right time on land, sheltering beneath the trees in the green, warm darkness in a port he no longer remembered. Not Dutch Harbour. Not Bergen. Maybe St. John's. Maybe Vancouver. Niechivo. It didn't matter, he decided.

His watch time was nearly upon him although there was still no light in the sky. He washed and dressed in the dark, closed the porthole and latched his door to the bulkhead so anyone might see he was not in his cabin. He walked up to the bridge and nodded to Viktor, who had worked as his helmsman through four voyages. He fixed the *Aleksei Chirikov*'s position on the chart and marked it in the log, then looked at the radar screen, which was cluttered with rain but gave no cause for alarm. The nearest vessel, a grain ship, was more than fifteen miles away. The closest land, Cape Lopatka at the end of the Kamchatka Peninsula, lay four days' running time to the northeast.

The second officer smiled at Viktor, touched his shoulder lightly, opened the portside door and went out onto the deck in the rain. The bridge door swung back and forth behind him, allowing Viktor to see him as he climbed the deck rail and balanced for an instant on its slick, rounded surface before he stepped off into the dark air and water.

The new second officer on *Aleksei Chirikov*'s summer voyage was put into the double cabin next door with the third officer, the same boy who had been on board the previous winter. Nearly all of the crew were the same. The other cabin was left empty.

Except for the motormen, the chief cook and the helmsman, everyone on board gathered on the boat deck and the wings of the bridge when the ship neared the latitude and longitude where the second officer had gone over the side. They had long since forgiven him for their lost fishing time and for the hours of useless searching through black water. Sasha, the deck bo's'n, still had the second officer's silver penknife, the tiny one from Odessa with flowers and leaves engraved on the handle. He had meant to return the knife the very day the man had drowned himself. Anna from the laundry had found a dark hair clinging to the pillowcase when she stripped the bedclothes from the second officer's bunk. She had shed a few secret tears, then confided them to Raisa Sergeyeva, still the ship's bufetchitsa, who told the pillowcase tale to others on board. One of the fishermen from the trawl deck was thinking of writing a song to commemorate the death of the second officer.

Despite these proofs of luxurious and satisfying grief, no one on the *Aleksei Chirikov* felt the second officer's suicide was mad, or even unreasonable. Those who stayed on shore might not know it, they thought, but the more remarkable situation on this or the last or any other voyage was that no others of the ship's company had decided to end the tension which arises in those who cling to an eggshell craft, remembering how smoothly the land rolls on without them, while determinedly keeping themselves separate from the sea. The sea who cradles us and pushes us away and reaches out for us. Sucking and roaring and yearning after us.

RICHARD CUMYN

The Sound He Made

This dope addict friend of mine, I had not seen him since the fall, heard that I had a kid and got hold of my phone number from my mother. Gayle and I were in a bachelor apartment in Lowertown then, subletting off a guy who moved back into his old house while his father wintered in Florida. Gayle was using the electric breast pump we were renting because the baby was not latching on properly. The first thing he said when I picked up the phone, he could hear the machine sucking in the background, was, "What is this Hill, I dial into an obscene call?"

I knew it was him right off. We had not seen each other for about eight months, not since the time he showed up at Miller House on a Thursday pub night and shared a cigarette with Gayle as we sat together at a table and watched student teachers dance to the Village People. The music was pretty lame. That was before I got Gayle to quit smoking.

Bam was what we called him from the time he collided with this white Citroen while riding his bike. It was the sound he made, like a gun going off, as he bounced off the hood. He didn't ask for his own cig, just kept sharing with Gayle like they were doing a private number together. He explained his nickname for her, rolled up his pant leg to show her the L-shaped scar in his calf where his front mud guard had gouged out enough meat to make a Big Mac. His words. I don't know what I did. I think I just looked away.

His real name is Mitchell O'Day. We met the summer we

34

were twelve years old and going to the same summer day camp, the one run by the civil service recreational association down on Riverside Drive. His father and my mother both worked at Supply and Services but didn't know each other. Due to the accident, Bam missed the middle session of the camp. When he started going again, he was supposed to be using a crutch but he always ditched it in this hollow tree in Vincent Massey Park first thing in the morning.

Early August sometime and we had been riding our bikes after dark, a bunch of us. Only one guy had a headlight, the kind that generates its own power against the front tire, but he never used it because he said it only slowed him down. Bam hit that Citroen like a gun going off. The driver didn't even stick around to see if he was all right. The guy with the headlight and I ran to get Bam's father. We were on his street, a dead end, just a couple of houses away, actually.

Last time we saw each other I had told him to find the nearest slimy rock and climb back under it. I guess that's what happens. A crowd of student teachers were doing the body language to "YMCA." It was a real education living there in residence that year with those teachers-to-be. It made me think seriously about home schooling but only in the abstract, though. Gayle and I had only made love the once. Bam didn't even know we were interested in each other and we had no idea how quickly things would progress. He must have had a feeling about us, though. It's not something you can hide very well. It just wasn't anything we had told anyone yet. As far as he was concerned, Gayle was just this very self-assured, sophisticated-acting honey sitting at the same table as he was. She was somebody to share a smoke with, bounce a few of his moves off of. I sat there smiling at his whole act.

He bled one bucket of blood. The bike had been run over, that was obvious from the way the frame was now operating in two planes instead of just one. Bam's father came running out with this sofa cushion in his hand, the first thing he had grabbed. Bam was sitting up hugging his knee to his chest. The whole pant leg of his jeans was soaked. Mr. O'Day stood there with this puzzled look on his face, turning the cushion over and over in his hands like he was trying to figure out some way to use it on the leg to stop the bleeding. Then he saw the wrecked bike in the middle of the street and he started yelling at the rest of us. That was how he dealt with it. His son had totalled his new BMX that had cost about two hundred dollars.

They were playing "Macho Man" for about the fifth time when one of the real idiots in our building, this nut who had decided to become a teacher after eighteen years of being an appliance salesman at Sear's, brought his Volkswagen into the building. He must have got all his buddies to help lift it up the stairs. We heard the motor running and turned around to look where people were pointing at the cafeteria windows behind us and there he was driving backward and forward in the hallway. Two student constables went out to try to stop him but couldn't really do anything except look stern and shake their heads the way their parents might in the same situation.

This was too much for Bam. He'd been working in the mail room of the Empire Life Insurance Company since high school and I could tell it was getting to him, draining him somehow. He wasn't even supposed to be with us. He'd just taken off at noon, driven all the way down, about a two hour drive, with no intention of making it back in time for work in the morning. "You got me for the whole fucking *fin de siècle*, Hill," he said. He meant the weekend but he actually went back home that same night.

Gayle was being too cool about him being there. I wanted her to give me a sign that it was time to head up for the night but she kept touching his arm when she spoke to him. When Bam saw the VW Bug outside the pub doors, he downed the last of his beer and Gayle's, too, and grabbed her by the hand. She laughed and almost stumbled trying to keep up. They ran out the door together and I went out behind them along with most of the rest of the pub.

We heard that the ex-salesman killed himself just before graduation. Not many people knew about it. They were all out trying to get hired. He was making this show of weaving close to the people in line who were waiting to get into the pub, making them think he was going to hit them. He skidded to a stop in front of Gayle and Bam. She was still holding onto his hand. In reflex she turned and buried her face into his chest.

It's hard to know what made Bam do what he did next. He has this streak in him. It made me think about him getting that Citroen driver back only a week after the accident. I don't even remember the asshole's name, only that he lived on Bam's street right where it ended, owned a chain of drycleaning outlets, and drove the only car of its make in the neighbourhood. Someone we knew said it was considered France's Rolls Royce. The guy wasn't really that old, forty may be. He lived all alone in this huge house. Every Sunday morning he washed his car. He loved that funny looking car, we could tell by the way he buffed it dry with a chamois before he waxed it. We played ball in the park at the other end of the street and every Sunday a stream of sudsy water ran down and soaked the area around first base. Bam would look up the street at the source of the stream and yell, "Frog Face!" He knew the guy could hear him.

The name, "Frog Face," started back in the winter. Any time we had a road hockey game going and the Citroen guy was coming home after work, instead of slowing down to give us time to move the nets over to the curb, he honked his horn impatiently to let us know that he had no intention of slowing down. The first player to see one always called, "Car!" any normal time and that meant one thing. Bam was the one who first yelled, "Frog Face!" at the Citroen and we knew that meant get out of the way as fast as humanly possible. We all began saying it. That was when it started between them. That was before Bam got his nickname.

Bam still had his stitches when he fixed that fucker's wagon but good. He never told Mr. O'Day who the driver was. He never even mentioned the car. The story he told his father, the one he made me and the other guys swear we'd stick to, was that old lady Billingham's yappy terrier had run out in front of him and he had to stop so quickly that he went right up over the handlebars. The next question was how had he bent the frame all to rat shit if all he had done was flip over the bars and how'd his leg get so cut up by the fender? Bam said it just did, he didn't know exactly how. It just did. His father let it be.

The phrase, "Frog Face," was all Bam, even when we started saying it and fitting it into dirty songs. He had nothing against the French but he had a powerful hate on for that drycleaner who washed his car so devotedly every Sunday. Even after we stopped playing road hockey and took to the ball diamond round about the first of June, whenever he saw the Citroen he yelled the insult loud enough the guy would have had to be deaf not to hear. When he drove past, he looked straight at us like he was trying to burn a hole right through our eyes. He would have killed us if he'd been able to get away with it, that was the message. He would have killed us, not despite but because we were children. He was an adult who lived across a gulf none of us could conceive of spanning. Ever.

The guy knew us to see us, we'd yelled, "Frog Face" and splattered his car with dirty salt slush enough as he drove by. But he didn't know Bam's cousin, Henry who was our age and lived on the other side of the city. Henry was over visiting with his little brother, Justin, the Sunday Bam got the guy back for running over his bike. I was in on it but never told anyone I knew a thing about it, not even after the shit called the police and made our fathers bring us down to the station to answer questions about it. Bam shouldn't even have been walking around, the risk of popping his stitches was still too great. But Henry's family was over visiting and it was this lush midsummer morning that made me think that it had to have always been that bright. At no time could it have been dark night. Bam had money from his paper route, five dollars, which Henry said he would split with Justin but we knew otherwise. We wouldn't have shared it either.

I would have done exactly what Bam did if I'd had the guts. It's what I was thinking when Bam lifted Gayle onto the roof of that Volkswagen: I wish I had thought of doing it first. It was such a commanding gesture. He put his two hands around her waist that she had been so proud of, barely 22 inches before I got her pregnant. She used to be proud of the fact that I could almost encircle her waist with my two hands. He boosted her up onto the roof of that car as if she was queen of the parade and he was king and this wasn't a car being driven inside a college residence by a drunken student teacher but the lead car in a grand football parade. Bam looked up at her, at his handiwork, this queen enthroned, and beamed. He opened himself all the way up smiling.

Gayle didn't know what to think, that was clear from her face. She gave me this pleading look as if to say, Who is this person you say is your best friend since you were kids? Who is he that he looks so pleased with himself? Not, Get me down from here. She was fully capable of sliding off quickly without much problem, although sometimes I think about her being up there and four weeks pregnant and neither of us knowing a thing about it. That was how green we were.

No, she stayed up there of her own volition but her look was full of these questions I knew she was demanding I answer. Explain Bam before another second passes, for one thing. That would have been something if I'd been able to do it. Explain Bam. That's a good one.

The guy who drove the Citroen, he might have been thinking the same kind of thing. He had no proof it was Bam who did that number on his baby, but a person would have to be a moron not to make the connection. You try to run over a kid out riding his bike at night and a week later the paint on one side of your car is burned off? It doesn't take genius.

Little Justin set up the distraction which wasn't difficult because he had no clue what was going on. I mean the kid was all of three years old. He loved to do just about anything there was to do with Henry and the little squirt loved to draw on things most of all. Bam gave Henry the fiver and a Coke bottle full of sulphuric acid that he'd funnelled from Mr. O'Day's basement workshop where he did plate metal etchings as a hobby.

"Don't get it on your skin," he told Henry, "and don't let Justin drink any."

Henry tapped his shoe in the stream of soapy water coming down the street and said, "What do you think I am, a moron?" Then he and Justin started hand-in-hand up toward the big house at the top of the street. Bam and I hid in Mrs. Billingham's cedar hedge where we took turns peeking through my father's field glasses.

I saw Henry bend down and whisper something in Justin's ear. If the guy saw them, he wasn't paying any attention to them. The little pecker scooted around to the side the man wasn't washing and began to go at the car with his coloured sidewalk chalk. Bam kept grabbing the binoculars from me. When I looked again, Henry had walked a way back down the street and doubled back, giving Justin time to draw one hell of a surreal mural on the driver's door, the wet colours smeared all over the place.

Then Henry walked up behind the guy, who was down in a crouch doing a hubcap. We got the full report.

He said, "Hey mister, have you seen my little brother around here?"

"No, I haven't," said the man without looking up. I imagine him thinking, Leave me alone, you little peckerhead, this is the only day of the week I have to relax.

Then he noticed the little pair of feet under the car and the sound of creative humming. "What the?"

I saw him come around the front of the car, where he saw Justin making his masterpiece, and bring his hand up to his forehead. Next thing, he hauled the garden hose around to that side and started hosing the colours off. Justin began to cry. The guy finished spraying, then crouched down so that he was level with the boy, trying to console him but that only made Justin cry harder. We couldn't see Henry who was around the other side of the car but we knew what he was doing.

What was it about Bam and cars? The guy driving the Volkswagen, the drunk, reached one hand up through his open window and grabbed hold of Gayle's leg, at the same time throwing the car into reverse. This was getting to be too much. I yelled for him to stop. Gayle was screaming at me. I looked at Bam who was laughing while he unbuttoned his shirt. The car shot forward, toward us again and Bam stepped into its path, waving his shirt in front of it. The guy slammed the brakes on hard, leaving rubber a good thirty feet past where Bam sidestepped it. When the car stopped, Gayle kept going, rolling down the windshield and hood and onto the floor like some crash test dummy without its seatbelt. Bam was still laughing. I ran to Gayle, got her to her feet. She was shaken and crying but unhurt.

Bam said to Gayle, "You have just experienced the ultimate rush, my dear."

I told him to shut the fuck up. Then I walked back to the car and kicked the guy's door in, I was so mad. When he heard the sound he roused himself and hung his head out the window. I'd put a sizeable dent in the middle of the door panel. He got out to inspect it. Someone said later that he had been drinking since early that morning. He'd got his first practice teaching report back and had received unsatisfactory ratings in all five evaluation criteria. The third day in the school he had put some punk up against a locker and started cuffing him in the head. The principal had advised him not to come back to that particular high school to teach.

He ran his fingers along the dent where I'd cracked the paint. I was ready for him to come over and pound me out. The engine was still running, it sounded like a rattling little tank. Someone told him to turn it the fuck off, he was going to asphyxiate us all, but he left it running. He walked around to the other side and hauled back and kicked the passenger door with the flat of his foot.

"There," he managed to say. "Equilibrium."

He actually stayed at the college longer than we did although, like us, he didn't graduate. He was directing the annual drama department production that year, Agatha Christie's *Mousetrap*. He put so much time into the play that he did nothing else. None of his media labs got done, none of his lessons were prepared. We heard that the play was a big hit, though.

Slowly and deliberately, the way people will when they are trying to sound sober, he said, "If someone will help me, I will remove this vehicle from the premises," as if the whole lot of us had just finished a dress rehearsal and he was putting the wraps on it, the final word. "If some of you would step forward. . . ." He was swaying forward and back. "If someone could just . . ." dropping off, losing his thought.

"It's all right, Bud," said Bam. "Don't worry. We'll help you."

About twenty of them lifted the Volkswagen down the stairs and out of the building for him. Though he hadn't damaged anything, he had to pay a fine for the violation. I was still angry at Bam for the way he scared Gayle and I told him so when he came back inside. He looked at me like I was crazy.

"You haven't got the hots for that one, do you? Her ass is too big. She's a cow."

I told him to find the rock he'd crawled out from and slide back under. I told him I never wanted to see his ugly face again. I could have killed the son of a bitch. Gayle never knew what he said.

"He's just like that," I said after he'd gone. "One minute he has plans with you and the next he's out thumbing his way across the country."

Gayle said, "I noticed he limps. Is that from the accident?" Jesus, after terrifying her half to death, he still had her conned! I could have killed him.

The Citroen guy lost skin off his right hand up to the middle of the arm and paint off the driver's side of his car. By the time he realized what had happened, Henry and Justin were gone and we made sure they stayed out of sight until it was time for them to leave. He came around that evening, his hand bandaged asking if we'd seen two boys that fit their description. He let us know by the way he looked at us that he knew what was going on. In September he put his house on the market and moved away.

He was out to kill Bam that midsummer night, though. The car's got those headlights that wrap around flush with the nose of the car. Bam knew it right away, even in the dark.

"Look," he said, "it's old Frog Face."

He stopped his bike smack in the middle of the street.

"Car!" he called, the way we did it in winter.

Instead of swerving around him, the guy stopped inches from Bam's wheel.

"Get out of the way, please," said the driver in this voice, this fatigued, condescending, hateful voice.

"Go around, Frog Face," Bam said. I couldn't believe it.

"Move your ass, kid, or I'll run it over."

"Go ahead."

The guy considered this for a minute and then backed down the street all the way to the park where we played ball. At first I thought he was going to turn around and go another way but he stopped, still pointed toward us.

"What's he doing? What's Frog Face doing, Hill?"

I said, "How should I know?"

Then the Citroen's high beams flipped on and he started cruising up toward us, not really giving it much gas, just letting the car find its own way up.

"He's not stopping," I said, squinting, from the curb. "Better get out of the way, Mitch." What did I know?

He stood up on his pedals, balancing, waiting. Then he released his brake and, still standing, began to roll down toward the car. Though he didn't pedal, he was picking up momentum faster than the car. The collision was stupid, just a stupid, avoidable thing. When Bam hit, he had lifted his front wheel right off the ground. I couldn't see all that well in the dark but the way it looked, he was as bent on attacking the Citroen as Frog Face was determined to roll unimpeded up that hill into his own driveway. It sounded like a gunshot. Bam hit, slicing his leg open on his own fender, and somersaulted the length of the car over its roof. The car kept on going straight, running over the bike on its slow, relentless march home.

When Bam arrived, Gayle was having a bath and the baby was asleep. He had three studs in his ear, big deliberate holes in the knees of his jeans. His Converse sneakers were two different colours, one red, one green. Port and starboard, he said. He was drunk. He dangled a champagne bottle by its neck.

"Where's this kid?" he said.

I showed him the baby asleep in its cradle.

When he opened the bottle, the cork flew across the room and hit our one and only print, a Bateman cougar, cracking the glass. I came back from the kitchen with two juice glasses. He filled mine to overflowing and took a chug from the bottle. Some of the carbonation backfired through his nose and he started laughing and sputtering.

He talked about what he was doing, working for a record distributor now. He had a company car, free concert tickets any time he wanted them, an expense account. He was making more money than his father.

"Most of it goes up my nose," he said.

For some reason he got to talking about this story his father had told him. Mr. O'Day used to work for a mining exploration company. Much of the electromagnetic work was done in the winter when they could get out onto the frozen lakes. It was tricky, though, getting up there. They had to wait until freeze-up to be sure it was safe enough to land the planes on the ice. Mr. O'Day was the leader of a group of eight men prepared to establish a base and run tests right through until spring thaw. His men were eager to get in there and start banking their isolation pay which would begin to be deposited the day they set up camp. The problem was that there had been a series of short freezes and thaws that fall and the ice was what they called candling. Mr. O'Day thought it wouldn't hold a plane. He stepped out onto the ice and showed them by ramming his axe handle down through the first crust. He wanted to wait another week.

The other men were not willing to wait. Mr. O'Day was replaced as leader. He was told that the plane was flying that day. He could come with them or stay. He thought about his wife and new baby that he had left so far away at home. If he had been single, he told his son, he would have risked it. They could probably run the plane on its skis as close to the shore as possible. If it started to go through the ice, the worst that would happen would be that they'd get wet and cold wading through the shallows. The balance was tipped, though, by the fact that he had two people back home depending on him. He decided to forfeit the isolation pay and stay put. There was nothing for him to do up there and so they shipped him home.

The plane landed safely and the crew had a successful winter. Their tests indicated the presence of a substantial ore body beneath the lake, what would become a lucrative mine. The man who took over from Mr. O'Day as crew foreman that winter went on to become a vice-president of the company.

"He said to me, he said, 'Mitchell, the night I drove you to the hospital, I was as frightened and angry as I have ever been in my life. I sat in that waiting room with your mother for five hours while they reattached the muscles and nerves in your leg and I wept. Like a little baby. Boy, it was as much for me as it was for you that I cried.' Doesn't that beat all, Hill?" said Bam.

I could hear Gayle's light splashing sounds coming from the bathroom and I knew she could hear us. When she takes a bath, she likes to let hot water from the sponge dribble down onto her face and chest. Bam talked and drank until the bottle was empty. I had the one glassful. Then the baby woke up hungry.

"I just fed him twenty minutes ago," I said.

I got a bottle of breast milk from the fridge and heated it up in a pan of water. Bam stood in the doorway of the kitchen and watched.

"You got it under control, don't you, Bud?" he said.

I had the kid on one shoulder and I was swaying from side to side, trying to calm him down while the milk warmed.

"I'll be on my way, then," he said.

"Thanks for dropping by," I said.

"Is that all, Hill?"

"I guess it is."

"So you went ahead and married her."

"That's what people do."

"Frog Face," he said.

When she heard the door close, Gayle said, "Come in here. You have to see this."

I opened the bathroom door. The water was level with the top of the tub. Her breasts floated on the surface.

"Watch this," she said. The baby had stopped crying for the moment and was rooting at my shoulder. Gayle lifted her breasts and twin jets of milk spurted out. "As soon as your friend came in, this started to happen. I was listening to you talk and these started going crazy. Look at this water now." It was all cloudy.

"I thought you were going to say, 'As soon as the baby started crying'."

"No, it was as soon as I heard his voice."

"Why didn't you get out and say hello?"

"I don't know why. I was starting to flow. It was nice. I didn't want to move."

"He drank an entire bottle of champagne himself. He looks . . . not so great."

"Then I'm glad I didn't get out. Here, hand him to me," she said.

"In the bath?"

"It's warm. Take his sleeper and diaper off." I undressed him and passed him down to her. "There. It's nice," she said.

It took a while for him to stop crying again. On the best of days he doesn't enjoy his bath in the little plastic tub we fill up on the kitchen table. Gayle played with him until he got used to the feel of the water. She held him so that he was half-floating, half lying on her stomach. Her milk was flowing so freely now that it was no effort at all for him to suck. They looked like sea mammals lying in the shallows, all sleek and pink.

"I'm glad I only listened and didn't come out," she said. "He is your best friend. I like to think about you having a best friend. Does it make you sad?"

I said, "Yes. Yes, I guess it does. He came over because he had heard about the baby."

"We'll see him again," she said," "What was that bang I heard earlier?" I told her about the picture.

When he had drunk his fill the baby fell asleep. The three of us stayed like that for a long time, me on the toilet seat, Gayle and the baby floating together in the steamy water. I didn't want to move.

MELISSA HARDY

Long Man the River

Shall we gather at the river,
Where bright angels feet have trod,
With the crystal tide forever
Flowing past the throne of God?

Well! I'd have reckoned that to be what you'd call a moot question, thought 'Liza Light-Up-The-Sky Talahawa, who was standing on the bank of the Ocunaluftee at nine o'clock on a Sunday morning in late autumn, cracking her knuckles apprehensively in grim expectation of her imminent total immersion in the river's icy water. The dull, pewter-coloured mist hugged the river like its ghost had not yet stirred and dissipated, but already the folks of Yellow Hill had collected on the shores of the Ocunaluftee to do their churching. Preacher Josiah Etowah had chosen to meet down here near Birdtown where the river shallows out instead of up in Yellow Hill on account of Peggie Whistle, the big-headed dwarf woman who stood with her armpits draped over a pair of Canadian crutches at 'Liza's side.

"I cannot undertake to drown any poor seeker after salvation in the ebullient and raging Blood of the Lamb," Josiah had explained to his parishioners – the Ocunaluftee up at Yellow Hill runs chin-high on a grown man.

On the margin of the river,
Waking up its silver spray,

> *We will walk and worship ever,*
> *All the happy golden day.*

Actually, it was more of what 'Liza would call a mizzling sort of day – just this side of rainy.

> *Ere we reach the shining river,*
> *Lay we every burden down;*
> *Grace our spirits will deliver,*
> *And provide a robe and crown.*

'Liza glanced back over her shoulder at the throng of parishioners who sat huddled and hunch-shouldered on blankets spread over the bumpy, sparse grass. *It's a moot question, seeing as how we're already gathered by the river,* she thought. Then she cracked her knuckles once again, speculatively but also nervously, making a dry, pod-snapping kind of sound, like the report of a distant bee bee gun – 'Liza could be as annoying as she was fine looking, big boned and lithe-tall in a rayon dress splashed with big flowers that hugged her figure like a lover.

> *Soon we'll reach the shining river,*
> *Soon our pilgrimage will cease,*
> *Soon our happy hearts will quiver*
> *With the melody of peace.*

Peggie, who enjoyed quite a reputation as a joker, decided to chat 'Liza up. "What did the Indian say to his neighbour after he watched Columbus disembark from his ship?"

"I don't know," said 'Liza, who hated jokes.

"There goes the neighbourhood!" Peggie retorted, hacking with dry laughter.

'Liza snorted contemptuously, as the congregation launched into the refrain:

> *Yes, we'll gather gather at the river,*
> *The beautiful, the beautiful river,*
> *Gather with the saints at the river*
> *that flows by the throne of God.*

"The only problem is that first it flows by the motels in downtown Cherokee," Peggie continued, wiping tears of laughter from her eyes with the back of one arm. "And the motels dump all the white man's sewage into it! *Heh! Heh!*"

'Liza stood, staring at the river, remembering foaming water, littered with red and yellow and brown leaves. . . . It was just as it had been when her father had made her go to water for the first time. Before she was aware of what she was doing, she began to comb the surface of the water for evidence of the creature which lived in these depths . . . for the broad streak of firefly green that betrayed its presence. Then suddenly she caught herself. *This rite is important,* she told herself. *You must try and keep control of yourself. Try not to let the others know.* In an effort both to reclaim and advertise her equilibrium, she feigned nonchalance: wrinkled up her fine, proud nose – it arched bonily like the back of a cat – and shook back her hair from her shoulders. Despite the fact that she was no girl, she still wore it long and black and loose to her waist.

Like Peggie Whistle 'Liza was here to be baptized, but not because she had seen anything resembling *The Light.* What she had seen was Walter Barkman, that white man who owned not only the Ocunaluftee Joke and Rock Shop down at the juncture of Highway 441 and Highway 19, but the adjoining laundromat and a photo-finish kiosk across the way as well. He was in one of his available phases right now. Women were forever taking up with Wally Barkman, then leaving him – so much so that folks lost count. (Also there was the problem that, his wives being for the most part white, there was no telling them apart.)

Well, 'Liza was dirt sick of being poor. Her husband of ten years, Ronnie Talahawa, had died two years this December leaving her with nothing but 223 purely worthless baseball cards, an eviction notice, and the selfsame handful of dreams she had walked down the aisle with a decade before . . . if you could call standing up in front of the Justice of the Peace of Swain County walking down the aisle. Died of an aggravated case of drinking sour mash. It was coming to him, all right; he'd been working on it for years, honing his self-destructive techniques to a pure perfection.

And those dreams she had brought to the marriage . . . they were all creased now and bent out of shape. However, all that would be set right again, once she had Wally Barkman firmly in tow. Lucky for her that she had not outgrown that gaunt, hybrid beauty – the high cheekbones and the bold nose and the big, strangely russet-colored eyes fringed with dark lashes which had once made her the talk of the Boundary. It had come to her down through her father, Joe Light-Up-The-Sky, whose family was descended from the Old Settlers out in the Oklahoma territory and was the result of the high incidence of intermarriage which had taken place in that no man's land nineteenth-century *unakas* called Indian Territory.

"Now, here's one," Peggie offered. "What was Custer wearing at his last stand?" Baited by the tall woman's dismissive attitude, Peggie could not resist the temptation to annoy her. She was like a cat that way. When she had been younger and more mobile, she had made a practice of biting people who ignored her about the ankles.

"I don't know," said 'Liza.

"An arrow shirt," Peggie erupted, cackling.

A gold Pontiac LeMans nosed into the shoulder of the road. Power brakes bit into the loose gravel, power windows rolled up, and Wally Barkman stepped out of the driver's seat onto the pavement. "Hi, Darlin'!" he waved. He held something . . . a cloth of some sort . . . draped over one arm.

Not properly a member of this congregation of Cherokee Baptists, he came no further but stayed where he was, up by the road – he leaned against the side of his big car and lit up a Camel cigarette.

Wally was fifteen years 'Liza's senior. He was bald, had a pink face spangled with golden freckles and a stomach that hung down so low that it covered his you know what even when he stood. Every time he wanted to do something with that thing, he had to haul his big stomach out of the way. He had come down to see her baptized – well, it was all his idea and doing, after all. Wally was one of those Born Again Christians, prone to lapses, forever on a wild yo-yo between

Salvation and Perdition, and right now he was on a redemptory swing.

'Liza swore under her breath. *Ka nu nu.* Bullfrog. She was riled. She felt as though a wide-toothed comb were being dragged down her spinal cord. Oh, she knew full well why Wally was here. He didn't trust her to follow through with her promise to embrace Jesus Christ as her saviour. He had come to make sure that she fulfilled her end of the bargain he had struck: Her rejection of Christianity had always been a point of pride with her. Alone of all her family she had followed Joe Light-Up-The-Sky in hating the white man's religion. "One of the things the white man gave the Indian was Jesus Christ," Joe used to say. "The other thing that comes to mind is smallpox." 'Liza wanted to scream and tear her hair and her clothes and jump all around like the crazy woman that she was inside, but instead, she just lifted her hand and smiled gently in his direction, as meek and mild as that fellow Jesus himself. In return, he lifted his pudgy hand in silent salute.

There is no territory so thoroughly negotiated as that dark boundary between a woman and a man about to bind themselves together for whatever measure of eternity will fall to their lot.

But now Preacher Josiah Etowah was shuffling towards 'Liza and Peggie in his worn hush puppies. His rusty black preacher's coat flapped open in the slight breeze that blew up from the river to reveal a black diver's wetsuit. Josiah was a big, untidy, stained man in his late thirties who always looked like his massive shoulders were a yoke too heavy for him to bear comfortably – he was forever moving and shifting them this way and that like he was trying to redistribute the weight somehow. He passed a battered Bible from one hand to the other like it was a football. "You ready for the symbolic death and resurrection of your soul, Sister 'Liza?" he asked in a ringing, adenoidal voice that did not sound natural in a man of his bulk – it sounded as if it were generated by some electrical implant.

'Liza glared combatively at him from under her fringe of lashes. "I reckon," she said.

"How about you, Sister Whistle?" Josiah turned to Peggie.

"Is the Pope Catholic?" Peggie quipped, poking at the toe of his hush puppies with the rubber tipped end of one of her crutches. "No, seriously, reverend, I've put the bean-bread out and the kettle on and I am ready to receive my Saviour with a heart full of joy and understanding," she assured him.

"Well, that's good . . . that warms my heart." Josiah turned to his congregation. "Brothers and sisters . . . hello, hello! Thank you for getting up this fine Sunday morning and coming all this way down to Birdtown to join us in the solemn baptizing of our sisters in Christ . . . I'm talking about Mrs. 'Liza Talahawa here who you all know and Miss Peggie Whistle. . . ."

In the meantime, Peggie was yanking at 'Liza's sleeve. "Hey! Hey!" she insisted. "Listen a minute. Now, this is a good one. Why were the Indians the first ones on the continent?"

"This is no time for joking around," 'Liza admonished her.

"Oh, the Lord likes a good laugh as well as anyone!" Peggie argued. "Otherwise how could He face another morning, with the mess He's made of things? Listen up now. They were the first ones on the continent because they had reservations!"

'Liza thought back to the first time she had become acquainted with Long Man the River: it had been when she was only a few weeks old.

Her father Joe wished his firstborn to be intelligent and to have a fine memory, so he engaged the services of Coming Back Teesatuskee, who was a conjure man. According to the ancient rite, Coming Back gathered burrs of the jimsonweed. Because burrs hold fast to any object they come in contact with, they therefore have the power to improve memory. Coming Back beat the burrs into a paste and mixed it with water taken from Mingo Falls, which is on the other side of Stoney Mountain Ridge. There were two reasons why he did this. The first is that a river seizes and holds fast anything that is cast upon its surface, as Joe wished 'Liza's mind to do. The second reason is that the noise of the cataract from which the water was taken is the voice of *Yunwi Gunnahita*, the river god. The water, therefore, contains within it lessons a child might absorb. He gave the mixture to Joe to feed 'Liza on four successive days.

After she had eaten Coming Back's mixture, 'Liza became very sick and almost died. Her mother, Ivy Light-Up-The-Sky, was fit to be tied. "That's it," she said. Her father had built the Yellow Hill Baptist Church. She had no use for conjuring save on those occasions when she needed a proper curse – Christianity is woefully lacking in the curse department. She packed Joe a bag and put it outside the cabin door. That meant divorce in Cherokee. From that day on, Joe no longer lived with them, though he often came up to the cabin to set a while with Ivy and visit with the girlchild who was to be his only spawn.

As for 'Liza, it was as though she had imbibed the god's voice at top volume and now there was no way of getting inside to turn that volume down. In any case, she could not remember back to a time when she did not hear a roaring in her ear or the whisper of hushed voices. And she remembered everything.

"Now, you know what the old song says?" Josiah Etowah reminded his congregation. "John the Baptist was a preacher . . . Some folks said he was a Jew . . . Some folks said he was a Christian . . . But he was a Baptist too!"

The congregation obliged him with a refrain:

> *I'm going to walk that lonesome valley!*
> *I'm going to walk it for myself!*
> *Nobody else can walk it for me!*
> *I'm going to walk it for myself!*

'Liza remembered that the first time she had actually gone to the water was when she was a little girl maybe eight years old. Now, *going to the water* is different from going down to the river. It's not a casual thing at all, and Cherokee have done it for as long as anyone can remember. *Going to the water* is a rite, like baptism in that it involves total immersion, but unlike baptism in that it is appropriate to many occasions – the rising of a new moon, for example, or the greening of the corn, or when a sickness is strong enough to call for strong medicine. *Going to the water* is not dependent on any change of outlook, but only upon a recognition of what is – Grandfather Fire, and the sun that the conjurors put up in the heavens because previously it had been too dark to see, and water, always water. These are the things that are.

It was 'Liza's father Joe who took her to the water: Big, handsome Joe with the profile off the backside of a nickel. He thought it might cure her of the whispering voices in her head, the constant roaring in her ears. It was late autumn at the time, as now, and, as now, leaves covered the surface of the river.

"This is good," Joe said. "The leaves give their medicine to the water. They make the medicine stronger."

"The water is too cold," objected 'Liza.

"Cold is only a feeling," Joe told her, taking hold of her underneath her armpits and plunging her into water so deep that her feet did not touch bottom.

'Liza came down with a chill, developed pneumonia, became delirious and for some time left her body, taking the shape of a raven. The period of her life spent as a raven she remembers in dreams. Upon her waking, these dry to a dust which settles imperceptibly all about her but through which all light is filtered.

Later, after she had recovered from her illness, her father fell from the suspension bridge to Saunooke's Village just beyond the Boundary Tree and drowned. His bloated, rock-battered body was found downriver, washed up in those shallows out back of the Drama Motel a couple of miles down Highway 441.

It is said that he was drunk, but 'Liza knew full well that he had been lured into the river by an *uktena*. An *uktena* is a giant serpent so dangerous that even looking at it might be enough to kill a person. Its body is as thick as the trunk of a tree, its scales glitter blue like ice in the moonlight, and on its antlered head shines a bright crystal, an *Uluhsati*. This crystal ensures its owner success in hunting, love, rainmaking, and,

most especially, in foretelling whether someone will live or die
– it is an object much sought after. It also so befuddles a man's
senses by its bright light that he cannot help but rush towards
it . . . and his own doom. Many men have died trying to possess
an *Uluhsati*, 'Liza's father Joe Light-Up-The-Sky among them.

Unfortunately *going to the water* had not cured 'Liza of the
voices in her head or the rushing sound in her ears. And the loss
of her father so cracked her heart that it became ever after a
fragile thing, subject to breaks.

"Yes, John the Baptist . . . he was a Baptist too!" repeated Josiah,
echoing the words of the song. "He was the first Baptist. And
why was he was a Baptist?"

"Because he baptized!" cried the congregation.

"And where did he baptize?"

"He baptized in the river!"

"And who did he baptize in the river?" cried Josiah.

"He baptized the Lord Jesus Christ in the river!" the congregation hollered back.

"Amen!" Josiah praised the Lord.

"Amen!" the congregation followed suit.

Shortly after Joe died, 'Liza began having those spells of hers.
Not all the time. Just some of the time. One minute Ivy'd be
talking to her, and she'd be listening, then other sounds would
start to creep in and gradually dominate her hearing – the
crunching sound of a female praying mantis chewing off the
head of its mate on the branch outside the window, the dull
thud of soil dropped from a gravedigger's spade onto the lid of a
coffin in a graveyard a quarter of a mile away, the wind in the
trees and the sound a distant fire sings to the brush as it eats it.

Or objects would lose their absolute definition and either
dissolve into a shimmer or become strangely fluent. Her
mother's chair would buzz busily away like a hive of electromagnetic particles. Floors would bubble and sway like
quagmires. Tables would heave and buck like the water in a
water bed when you jump on it. Actual water, on the other

hand, became as thick and metallic in its texture as mercury. The sound droplets made hitting a hard surface were as loud and jarring as a bucket of brass balls poured from a bucket onto the floor of a high school gymnasium.

But what was even more overwhelming was that, when a spell was come upon her, she began to experience a life in everything. She could hear the groans of the grass as it strained to grow up through the soil. She could feel as a hard knot in her chest the alarm of a bear which sensed her walking downwind of the cave in which her young were hidden. Most peculiar of all, the eggs in her body spoke with her familiarly and called her *Mother.*

Coming Back had taken her down to the water again, this time at Ivy's behest – she simply did not know what to do with the girl who would rise in the wee hours of the night and go reeling around the cabin like a drunk, trying to pinpoint in a vortex of shadow the location of the mysterious glittering object which haunted her dreams. "Get back to bed, 'Liza!" her mother would holler – thin shrill voice in the gloom. "There are eight people sleeping in this cabin! You're waking folks up!"

So the gaunt old man with the long, yellow-white hair had rattled beads and noted the movement of fish and admonished his patient to concentrate, *concentrate*, but it is an altogether different matter to fix the attention of an infant and of someone who is no longer a child. It involves tabus which must be observed for up to seven days, and 'Liza at the moment was incapable of focus. Then, towards the end of her time with Coming Back, she started to her feet and pointed to the river.

"Sit down, 'Liza!" Coming Back ordered. His voice was weary. How this girl tried his patience.

"But it's an *uktena*!" 'Liza cried, pointing. "There! Below the surface!"

"Send the *uktena* to the river below the river," Coming Back instructed her – for there is a world below this, like ours in every respect, except that there the seasons are different. The streams which come down from the mountains are the trails to that world. "Send the *uktena* home," he said. He had had enough of this crazy teenage girl. He wanted the money and the two pullets Ivy had promised him and to be done with it. Crouching by a damp river for several hours the past few days had aggravated his rheumatism to the point where he felt as though he had been flayed and then locked inside the stiff exoskeleton of a crawdad with instructions to escape as best he could.

But 'Liza had run to the shore and stood poised on the bank, peering into the water at the lithe body which coiled and uncoiled as fluorescent as a jewel between the dark green waters.

"Why did you take my father?" she cried.

But the *uktena* did not answer but only swam deeper until all that bespoke her presence was a green glow in the depth of the river.

'Liza stamped her foot and cursed and cried.

And from that time on, not only had 'Liza heard voices in her head and a roaring in her ears, not only did she fall into fits, but she also was quarrelsome. For it is a well-known fact that anyone who loses their temper when they are *going to the water* will be quarrelsome for the rest of their lives.

"Are you ready, Sister Talahawa?"

"What?" 'Liza snapped.

"Are you ready for holy baptism?" It was Josiah Etowah, inclining towards her.

"Oh, I 'spose," said 'Liza ungraciously, apprehensively. She glanced quickly towards the road at Wally Barkman. The owner of the Ocunaluftee Rock and Joke Shop still leaned against the Pontiac with his arms folded across his chest and a cigarette poking out of his mouth. He nodded by way of acknowledging her glance and made a flicking motion with the fingers of one hand as if to urge her forward. She turned back to Josiah. "Let's get this over with," she said and took the steadying hand he offered her.

Together preacher and convert negotiated the rocky bottom of the river like dancers navigating a crowded ballroom until they had reached its cold centre. 'Liza was numb, white-lipped with cold and dread. She knew for a certainty that the *uktena* was in the river. Why should she not be? She lived in the river. She had always lived in the river. And 'Liza was afraid of the *uktena*. So afraid. Peering downstream, she thought she detected movement and a glimmer of light, firebug green, below the water's leafstrewn surface. The blood blew through her veins like a firestorm, and she tried to pull her hand free of Josiah's.

"Come on, now," he said. "It's almost over," and, placing one hand firmly upon her head, he said, "Take a breath now," and shoved it underwater.

She saw the *uktena* then, saw her clearly, the powerful, languorous body draped in a loose coil about her feet, the iridescent sheen of her plated scales, the yellow headlamps of her eyes. The creature rubbed against her leg as seductively as a cat.

Josiah was pulling on her, trying to get her to surface, but she resisted him.

Why did you kill Joe Light-Up-The-Sky? 'Liza demanded of the *uktena*, but in her head, not with words. *Why did you kill my father?*

This time the *uktena* replied, also not with words. She spoke on the inside of 'Liza's skull in a language of tones: *I have no agenda apart from opportunity*, the *uktena* assured her. *Like any creature, I take what I can when it is offered me by the means I have at my disposal. In this I act no differently than you. Come. See this uluhsati I wear in my forehead?*

And, turning, she thrust the bulging crystal embedded in the cavity between her eyes towards 'Liza's face. It was as roughly faceted as a thing found in nature and gave off a glow that was more milky than bright.

Josiah yanked at her. She could hear him calling to her through the thickened water. "Mrs. Talahawa! Mrs. Talahawa!" She tried to twist away from his grasp.

If you pluck this from me, you will have success in love and in hunting . . . in all matter of things, the *uktena* assured her. *It is what your father wanted too.*

'Liza had just reached her hand out for it when Josiah reached underwater and, seizing her by the chin, dragged her face up into the air. 'Liza coughed and choked.

"What do you think you were doing? Why did you fight me? If you want to drown yourself, do it yourself!" he hissed angrily. With more force than was strictly necessary, he shoved her towards the shore. She stumbled on the slippery rocks and almost fell.

In the meantime, Peggie Whistle was scrambling crutch over crutch towards the road like a stifflegged quadruped, screaming, "Not me! I've changed my mind! Did you see? That preacher almost drowned her! No! No! Salvation is not worth dying for!"

Wally Barkman threw his cigarette down, ground it into the gravel, and, adjusting the object draped over his arm, started down the hill towards the bank of the river. When 'Liza stumbled ashore, spent and soaked and trembling, he stepped forward and spread the object wide. In this way, he took possession of the Indian woman who, at the very moment of her baptism, had been engaged in conversation with a river monster: took possession of her with a red, green and white striped Hudson's Bay blanket.

After her baptism, 'Liza took a chill and for a time was very ill. When she recovered, she married Wally Barkman. However, she never did get rid of the voices whispering inside her head or the roaring in her ears and, when she woke into the darkness of her night, it was always with fingers spread and tense, straining to grasp the bright crystal so close to hand and wrench it free.

ROBYN SARAH

Accept My Story

Melanie fell off the fire escape during one of the times she was living with Paula. She broke her leg and both hips and did something to her spinal column, and when they discharged her from the hospital ten months later, she walked with two canes and a brace, and they told her she was lucky to be alive.

People who knew her history were more careful about what they told her; even behind her back they never came out and said it, but they had their suspicions about the accident. How, they asked themselves (and their glances asked each other) do you *fall off* a fire escape? And it wasn't as though she'd never threatened. But Melanie said it was an accident, she was watering some plants, she said, that she and Paula had hung up there to brighten the view out the kitchen windows, and she lost her balance. It could have been true.

It could have been true, and I have accepted it as true, because I think of Melanie as a truthful person. I imagine it this way: a Saturday morning in mid-May, very fine and bright, the leaves at different stages of opening, still greeny-gold and frilly, the air fragrant and pleasantly cool; sweater weather. On Saturdays Paula likes to sleep in till nine-thirty or ten and then to have a leisurely, festive breakfast; knowing this and wishing to please, Melanie – who moved in three weeks ago – has slipped out at nine and gone round to the Patisserie for chocolate croissants; has selected two perfect oranges (re-wrapping them tenderly in their tissue paper) from the specialty fruit stand next door, and has come in quietly, fed the cats, and put on coffee. She's setting things out on the table when Paula pads in, barefoot, holding closed a man's terry robe torn at the shoulder. With her frizzy straw-coloured hair standing out in odd peaks and her eyes still sleep-crinkled, she looks preoccupied and severe.

"You're up early, Mel," she says. "What did you get? Oh, chocolate rolls, terrific. What are these?" She touches one of the oranges swathed in purple tissue.

"Those are the most *wonderful*-looking oranges," Melanie cries, and then, swooping to demonstrate, "I had to unwrap at least two dozen of them before I picked these two – they were *all* so gorgeous – and I think the girl thought I was crazy. Look, Paula!" She unwraps one and holds up the vivid fruit, pointing to where the glossy peel is marbled with crimson. "I've never seen these before, have you? They're from Italy. The girl says she only has them at this time of year, beginning around Easter. I couldn't *believe* the colour – especially in the sun. . . ."

"Blood oranges," says Paula. "That's what we used to call them. Or 'passion oranges.' They're flecked with red like that all through the insides, too."

"*Blood* oranges," Melanie repeats with a dubious giggle. "But the reason I got them, when I saw them I thought of that line from the Wallace Stevens poem – 'Late coffee and oranges in a sunny chair' – that's all I can remember of the poem, you know? but it sounded so delicious to me, coffee and oranges in the sun."

Sun pours across the table now. It's really the saving grace of Paula's small kitchen in this St. Urbain Street apartment, that it gets the morning sun, for the tall windows don't look out on much. They give on an inner courtyard, facing identical windows across the way and a network of black iron fire escapes, accessible by a slatted platform below sill level. Last week, when the weather began to be nice, Paula bought some flats of begonias and impatiens from in front of one of the grocers on St. Lawrence Street, and she and Melanie potted the plants individually and hung them at different levels on the fire escape.

"We could even eat outside," Melanie says. "We could take some big cushions out on the platform, and sit in the sun."

"Not my sofa cushions," Paula says sternly, and goes off to dress. When she comes back, the coffeemaker is hissing, the windows are open, and Melanie is out on the fire escape, watering the plants. "Come see!" she calls, leaning over the rail to reach a hanging pot, "the whosits are opening, not the ones with the furry leaves. The other ones. They're pink and white." And those are the last words she says before she comes to, in the hospital, nearly a week later.

I imagine Paula, whom I never met, as being stoical, brusque-mannered, tough. Making a point of her independence. But at the same time, tacitly dependent on Melanie for certain things – for a kind of liveliness; maybe for a sense of purpose. Say when Paula was twenty-three, the age Melanie is now, she gave a baby up for adoption, something she never talks about. Say she loved the father, a jazz musician several years her senior, but he couldn't handle the idea of a child at that point in his life; say he left when she refused to terminate the pregnancy, say in the end she signed the papers for love of him, for need of him, and in the very doing discovered that she had to leave him. Say all this happened in the United States, maybe somewhere in the midwest; and to pull her life together she fled to Canada, to Montreal, and found a job as secretary at the YWCA – where one night she found Melanie, a fifteen-year-old would-be runaway, hiding in the washroom.

It isn't hard to see how her apartment would soon become Melanie's home away from home, and later, when Melanie was working and could share the rent, how it would become her actual home on a few occasions, each lasting several months. In between, probably, there were boyfriends – Melanie's, Paula's. The two of them have to laugh at the way events in their separate lives fall out, time and again, to make roommates of them. "Paula, it's me. It's Melanie. Rick and I broke up. I can't afford this place alone. Can I stay with you till I find something cheaper?" Paula is always glad to have her, always says, "Sure, why don't you just move in? It'll save us both money." It is the third time – Paula has recently broken for good with a married man who went back to his wife one time too many; Melanie has just received, in a lump sum, a student loan to go to summer school and complete her high school leaving – that the accident happens.

"Accident."

"Happens."

It's funny how clearly I can see Paula, given I'm making her up, given that however I rack my brain, I can remember nothing that Melanie told me about her, except that she was older, had been married, kept cats. I see Paula: fair-skinned, hazel-eyed, curly-haired – I see her lean but wide-hipped, partial to western style jeans worn with a belt, mannish shirts and hats, shirt-style dresses for work. She's without vanity, wears no makeup, but she is scrupulous about skin care, treating her face each night with hot towels and a camomile astringent to open and close the pores. After doing this, her face looks splotchy and sensitive till bedtime; Melanie's olive skin is her envy.

I see her as Melanie sees her, at home, her guards down. She walks around barefoot; smokes, but not excessively; reads murder mysteries to unwind. She turns on the radio to hear the news or late-night jazz that she hums along with, making tortured jazz faces, as she catches up with neglected housework, or chops veggies for a spaghetti sauce she's cooking ahead, for company on the weekend, or for the freezer for a busy week to come. She has a TV but watches only the rare movie; she lets Melanie keep the TV in her room. In her voice a faint midwestern twang still resides, and in her speech, certain midwestern idioms. She doesn't smile a whole lot. ("A whole lot" is something she would say.) She doesn't talk a whole lot either, and what she says comes out dry and lightly ironical, an habitual tone of hers, self-deprecating, unsentimental. Melanie is used to it; herself given to effusions, she simply effuses, oblivious. They make an odd counterpoint, the two of them, in conversation.

I can see the cats, too, a pair of Siamese females named Lily and Nessa, a mother and daughter. Nessa is a little larger and that's the only way Melanie can tell them apart, though Paula insists their personalities are quite distinct. Lily, as a kitten, was a gift from the married man during the early days of his courtship of Paula; Paula had her bred because it didn't seem fair to get her spayed before she'd had a litter. She sold the other kittens for what sounds to Melanie like a fortune, and kept Nessa; then shipped Lily off to the vet. Nessa wasn't granted the same grace; she was shipped off right after her first heat. "*Why?*" asks Melanie. "You could have got *rich* doing that." But Paula only shrugs, blowing smoke rings, and says, "Too much hassle."

In the years since she met Melanie, Paula has forged ahead. She's taken management courses at night, has gone from an administrative position at the "Y" to a position as co-director of a local multicultural community project. She has learned French and spent a summer in Greece. Her loans are paid off, she's kept the apartment on St. Urbain because the rent is cheap, she's saving her money to buy a house. Melanie is wide-eyed at all of this. In the same period, she has been through several personal crises, three psychiatrists, a couple of love affairs (one of them with the second psychiatrist), four months as an in-patient, and more jobs than she can remember. She has gone from little pink pills to big white pills to amber capsules to no pills and back to little pink pills; from pills that made her feel stupid to pills that gave her tics and twitches, pills that made her hyperventilate and pills that closed up her throat during the night so that she'd wake choking. But Melanie has also audited university courses with the latest boyfriend, and has decided she wants to go to school "for real" if she can just get her high school leaving. She wants to study English litera-ture; for years she has written poetry that Paula thinks is "darn good."

Sometimes Paula knows, admits to herself, that Melanie is her child in a way, is a fast-forwarded version of the baby girl she relinquished – come to her by a miracle, returned to her so soon, already a woman, yet with an infant's fierce needs, a child's unconditional acceptance. But Paula is not given to this sort of thinking. If she feels an unreasoning anger when after a few months, on some whim, Melanie says she's moving out, Paula attributes it to Melanie's character: the girl is fickle and irresponsible. She doesn't need psychiatrists; she needs a good kick in the pants. Look at her, she's messy and undisciplined and plain lazy. So let her go. It will be nice to have the space again. And after a week or two during which the emptiness is so acute that Paula paces the floor at night, forgets to eat dinner, bites her nails to the quick – eventually it is.

I think of Melanie as a bit of an *enfant terrible*, but somehow invulnerable. In a way she's much tougher than Paula, though she is much more gullible, naive, overtly feminine. She has going for her that her own life and doings and what befalls her are intensely interesting and surprising; she has that detachment. It's her gift. She can always stand back from herself, her own life is like a very good novel, or the soaps. It never bores her. She is not at all inclined to self-pity or bitterness, does not bear grudges; she's generous in her interpretation of others. Paula still thinks she should go after the second psychiatrist, take the thing to court, he oughtn't to have been able to get away with that; but Melanie won't consider it: "I couldn't do that to him," she says, "the poor guy. I mean, he has kids and everything. Do you think a man like that can help himself? I was just stupid." She can seem a scatterbrain, but there's a saving intelligence underneath, that gets her out of scrapes just in time, or that allows her to forgive herself her errors, pick herself up, and move on.
Pick herself up. Did I say that?

But yes, that's how I've imagined it, imagined her. For really this Melanie, this adult Melanie, is as much an invention of mine as the Paula I've pulled out of the air, pulled together from fragments of other women I've known, bits of their stories. I scarcely knew the adult Melanie. I knew a child: my best friend in grades two and three, then an absent friend, when she moved with her parents to an outlying suburb in grade four. A voice on the telephone, almost nightly for a year or two (when we both still lived for rare weekend sleepovers), but less and less often over the years as we formed new friendships, became entrenched in our separate lives. Dimly, through the self-absorption of adolescence, I heard from my mother, who sometimes spoke to her mother, of Melanie's first breakdown. But it was unreal to me. Melanie, on the occasions when she phoned, still sounded like Melanie to me, and she was circumspect about her troubles, whatever they may have been. "Did you hear?" she might ask, as if in passing. "Did your mother tell you? No, but I mean, did she *tell* you? That I'm Seeing A Psychiatrist?" Sigh-*ky*-atrist, she pronounced it, with theatrical emphasis; then a stream of embarrassed giggles. What did I think, she'd want to know. Not knowing what to think, feeling I was being tested, I'd murmur something cautious, something I hoped was encouraging. More giggles. And then, perhaps, "He's really cute. Do you believe me? My sigh-*ky*-atrist, I mean. I see him twice a week. Tuesdays and Thursdays. He's a doll, no kidding!"

The week I started university was the week Melanie went into hospital. I remember that, because she phoned me – she phoned to wish me luck, wistful, vicariously excited – and I felt what a gulf had opened between us, how different our lives had become and were to be. I remember the constraint I felt during that conversation, the relief of putting the phone down. Melanie never asked me to visit her. I never thought of it. We hadn't seen each other for years, at that point, anyway.

Later there was a summer, part of a summer, when she roomed with me: she'd found a job downtown, near the university, and I had an apartment near there; one of my roommates was going to be away for a month and wanted to sublet her room to save money. I forget how it came about, whether Melanie phoned, or whether I ran into her, just at the moment when she was looking for a place and I was looking for a roommate. Anyway she moved in. I was a little nervous about it, but she got along well with the others – shared my room for the first two weeks till Jan left, then settled into Jan's – finding everything greatly to her liking and exuding an infectious, if slightly overwrought, enthusiasm for our menage in all its details.

There were three of us on the lease, and when Jan came back, Melanie wanted to stay on – to sleep in an alcove by the entranceway that could be closed off with a curtain, and to pay a quarter of the rent. The others concurred, but four in the house sounded like more chaos than I could handle during the school year, so I argued against. No, be honest: it was Melanie herself, and what I knew of her past, that gave me pause; and though I didn't say it, the others sensed it and came hotly to her defense. There was some unpleasantness, and finally *I* moved out, to a bedsitter of my own, and Melanie took my room and signed the lease in my stead. I heard several months later that it had ended badly, with pots and pans flying and a fist-fight over rent owing. I felt vindicated.

And after that, I saw her only once, in maybe my second year of graduate school, something like that. She called, she'd got my number from my mother, she was going to be in the neighbourhood, could we have lunch? It was mid-April, term-paper season for me, but I figured I could take an hour off. We agreed to meet on a certain corner, near a restaurant we both knew and had frequented during the apartment summer.

"You may not recognize me," she warned. "I'm shorter than I used to be."

"You're what?"

"*Well.*" The dubious giggle. "I had an *accident.* But I'll tell you when I see you. I just thought I should warn you, so you won't be shocked."

She was, in fact, about four inches shorter. She'd had some vertebrae removed, making her short-waisted. She was heavier, too. She came limping towards me on her canes and only the absolutely unabashed, unfeigned delight of her smile – a smile I could see from half a block away – got me through the awkwardness of our greeting. "I fell," she volunteered. "Last spring. I fell off a fire escape. I just got out of the hospital a month ago."

In the restaurant we ordered club sandwiches and milkshakes, our old standard, and she told me a little more. She'd been living at her friend Paula's when it happened. Had she ever told me about Paula? She hadn't? That was funny, because she'd lived with Paula a couple of times before. Paula was a divorcée – a lot older, but she was a really good friend. She was a character. She had (and now I remember it wasn't Siamese cats at all, it was dogs, little dogs) Pomeranians, had I ever seen a Pomeranian? Paula had two of them, they were "just the most *adorable* things." The limp was permanent. She'd had three operations. She would never walk without a cane.

Melanie amazed me that day, by her seeming equanimity at the prospect of living the rest of her life partly crippled, in her misshapen body; by her improbable cheerfulness. She surprised me, too, by apparently harbouring no hard feelings towards me, or anybody else, over the apartment episode: she asked after our former roommates in genuine interest, and had only nice things to say in remembering each of them. "Jan's in *law* school? You're kidding! *Gee*, I liked that girl. She was so *original!*" Once or twice, in response to things I said, she let out a scream of laughter that made people at adjoining tables look over our way, and I felt a wave of embarrassment, a desire to escape. I remember trying to tone things down, asking her about her ten months in hospital, how could she have stood being in there so long? But this evoked the same scream of laughter. "I loved it! The hospital was *wonderful!* I know it sounds crazy, but I had a wonderful time. Everybody there was so good to me, and they all said they liked me so much, and how brave I was, and everything. They made me feel so special! On the day I left they made a big party for me and everybody was crying. I never wanted to leave, Ruth, honest. I'm telling you, I could write a book about what it was like in that place, everybody that I met and all."

Oh, Melanie. How easily I believed you, how badly I must have needed to. "You should do that," I said, getting up to put my coat on and fishing my change-purse for a tip. "You always wrote so well." I was thinking of her grade-school compositions that the teacher always read out loud, and of the occasional poems and stories she'd shown me or read to me over the telephone, over the years.

"Gee," said Melanie, also getting up – it seemed to take her a long time, and I wondered if I should help her, but felt awkward to offer. She managed by herself. "Gee, do you really think so, Ruth? You think I could?"

"I really do."

"Gee," she repeated in a happy voice, as if turning it over. "Maybe I will."

Not long after this exchange, and not without trepidation, I married a fellow graduate student with whom I'd had a somewhat stormy but intense relationship for a couple of years, and moved with him back to his home town on the west coast, where we both soon found teaching positions. His was a tenure-track university post, in the History Department; but mine was a one-year contract, with renewal contingent on my finishing my M.A., which I'd shelved. Anyway mine was short-lived, because our daughter was a born a year after I was hired, and I got pregnant again while still on maternity leave and had another little girl fifteen months later. Murray and I held things together for a number of years, probably longer than we should have; we split up when the girls were five and six – both finally in school – and after a few months' separation I came back east with them to be nearer my parents, and by chance got a pretty good job in a theatre box office. I don't mean great pay, it's not; but good because the people are interesting, and I get free tickets to all the shows, and they lay me off in the summers so I can collect unemployment insurance and be home with the girls. Murray takes them for a week at Christmas and for three weeks in August – pays their plane fare – and he's been pretty good with the child support, I can't complain. It's not perfect but I really can't complain. Not compared to other women I've known.

During the whole time I was on the west coast, I wasn't in touch with Melanie. I spoke to her only once more – very shortly after my return. Again, it was she who called; again she'd got my number from my mother, who filled her in on where I'd been and what I'd been up to and why I was back. Melanie had some reason for phoning, something about wanting to enroll in university and thinking I'd be a good person to ask advice on which courses to take. She'd met someone, she told me; she was living with him, it had been a few years, but they weren't married. He was a salesman of some sort, he thought it would be good for her to do something with herself, because she got depressed when he was on the road. She hadn't been able to work since her accident, but she thought she could manage school.

At the time, I was too depressed myself to have much to say. It was nice to know that Melanie had found somebody, that she was looked after. It was also nice that she didn't ask anything about Murray. Actually, she'd met him – it was during the apartment summer that I'd begun seeing him – and in fact it was he who'd been behind my decision to move out of "that cloister" as he called it, and away from "those giddy school-girls." Melanie did ask, wistfully, what my daughters looked like. She was thrilled that I'd had children; she never would be able to, now. (I remember being startled by that, I hadn't put it together. When we were kids, we used to talk about the children we were going to have when we grew up, we even had their names all picked out.) She hinted that she would love to see my girls, and I think that I said something lame about maybe once I was more settled and had found a job. I wasn't up for seeing people much, those days, and Melanie, with her air of girlish expectancy and her willingness to admire me, was one person I knew I couldn't handle seeing at all – not right then. I took down her phone number, but on a piece of paper, not in my phone book; and subsequently I lost it. I never heard from her again.

Nor will I, because I found out last week that Melanie is dead. She died three and a half years ago, in early December – oddly enough, on the same day that the court heard my declaration for divorce. I know it was that day because I looked the date up, I wanted to place it somehow; ever since Caitlin was born, I've kept my old calendars. There it was, a Wednesday, circled, with "Court hearing, 9:15 a.m." written underneath. So I can picture the day exactly: it was heavily overcast, sombre; it hadn't snowed yet, because I remember I was wearing shoes, not boots, and walking down St. Antoine to the courthouse, my feet were cold. Murray was waiting just inside the main doors, smoking. He was on some sort of semester leave to do research for a book, so he'd been able to come east and co-file with me, saving lawyers' fees. He was staying with old school friends, and seeing the kids some – not as much as they'd expected, though, and not very reliably – and we weren't talking to each other much because at the last minute he'd stuck me with all the paperwork for the divorce (we were supposed to share it) saying he couldn't do that *and* see the girls and keep up with what he was supposed to be doing on his book. I was mad about that and about his cavalier scheduling of visits, based always on his convenience and subject to cancellation on short notice, leaving me to pick up the pieces. I remember on that day, the day of the hearing, he looked haggard and ill at ease; he had dark circles under his eyes and I noticed he also had deeply etched creases around them that were new, that I hadn't registered before. If he had even once looked at me directly, I might have felt compassion towards him, but he didn't, he made sure never to meet my eyes. There was a short wait in a crowded, smoky hallway where people were milling around a notice sheet to check their names on the list, and then we were called in.

The whole thing took all of about three minutes. I'd been prepared to defend our agreement if necessary, I had three typed pages of notes ready, but the judge never questioned us. Did we want to waive the thirty-day delay, he wanted to know. Taken by surprise, I glanced at Murray, who said, expressionless, that it was all right with him. So I said yes too. The judge declared us divorced, effective immediately, ordered us to respect the terms of our agreement, and we were ushered out before I'd had a chance to realize what had happened.

This was the "new" divorce; do-it-yourself, short-order divorce. It was supposed to spare people a lot of the pain and expense and nastiness of the old divorce. Instead it left me feeling the strangest kind of emptiness, at once as though nothing at all had happened and as though I'd been robbed. What, was our whole marriage, our life together as parents of two children, our decision to end that, and the hard work of finding our footing apart, something to be dismissed in three minutes? Should we not have been required to stand up and account for ourselves, to plead "Accept my story"? Weren't we entitled to have it acknowledged publicly that what we were doing was a serious thing? Or what were we doing there?

I didn't think any of this in so many words at the time – I just felt funny, unreal – left hanging, or as though I'd stepped out into empty air. We came down in the elevator silently, and at the door I asked Murray if he wanted to go get a cup of coffee somewhere, because it felt so abrupt the way it was, but he said in an abstracted voice, "No, I think I'll pass." So we shook hands on the street, a little formally (even then he wouldn't meet my eyes) and turned in our separate directions. I walked up to Ste. Catherine and along there to my bus stop, the sky was leaden and oppressive, Christmas decorations were up in all the store windows. I came home and felt (I'd asked for the day off, thinking we might have hours to wait, but I was home by ten-thirty) – I felt, the only word for it is "nothing," I felt "nothing," like a vacuum of feeling, all day. I remember the house was very dark, but I didn't feel like turning any lights on. I sort of folded myself into an armchair by the window and read – this is silly, but I read *Heidi*, because it was there, on the arm of the chair, Caitlin had it out of the school library. So I read *Heidi* – the whole thing.

At four-thirty, when the schoolbus was due, I walked out to the end of the next block to meet it where it stopped, and suggested to the girls that we go downtown to look at the store windows and then to a restaurant for an early dinner, pizza or Kentucky Fried, whichever they preferred. It was a transparent move on my part. Caitlin asked right away, "Did you go to court this morning with Daddy?" (had I really expected her to forget?) – and, when I said yes: "Are you divorced now?"

I said yes again, in a voice that came out inadvertently squeaky, and then Bronwen, bursting into tears, cried, "Well, I think that was a *stupid* idea!" and broke away from my reaching arms to run ahead. She ran all the way home; when we caught up to her she was on the porch, kicking savagely at the locked door, but she'd stopped crying. Later we went for Kentucky Fried.

Sometime that afternoon, across town, Melanie left the apartment she shared with the salesman I never met, walked five blocks to a similar apartment building on the other side of the Expressway, entered the building, somehow gained access to the roof, and jumped.

I happen to be a rememberer of birthdays and anniversaries, of special dates; I'm a believer in the significance of dates. So the coincidence of dates, though odd, was no surprise to me – nor did it seem strange that it was on Melanie's birthday I learned of her passing.

It was a coincidence and not a coincidence. The coincidence was the postcard that arrived that day from Murray's sister Nora in Vancouver, apologizing for not having answered my last two letters. The card explained she'd been too upset to write ever since Tom, a former lover who'd remained her dear friend, "jumped out a window, taking his leave of us dramatically."

I'd been close to Nora during the years Murray and I were together on the coast, and I stayed close to her after we separated, because Nora had been through a divorce herself and helped me out a lot during those first months, before I moved back east. We've corresponded since. Nora was the single soul who supported me in my decision – the decision to move back east – going against Murray and his parents and what all the pop-psychology books advised. "Ruth," I remember her saying to me as I anguished over it, "Look after yourself first. Think about *you*, stop thinking about everyone else, forget other people. What I'm hearing from you is a lot of second-guessing, what's right for the children, Murray, Gram and Gramps, everyone but the cleaning lady. You need to do what's right for *you*, Ruth. You need to go down into yourself and listen to your deepest inner voice. Just keep going lower – Get into the elevator and hit the 'DOWN' button. It'll stop on every floor, but keep going one lower."

What *wasn't* a coincidence was that I'd been thinking of Melanie all day – it was her birthday, that's why; I'd had to write a cheque that morning, and as I dated it, my special-date bell went off: Ding! *Melanie's birthday.* So she was on my mind. It was on my mind to try and get in touch with her again. I'd tried before: there comes a time, in the wake of divorce, when one looks to reconnect with one's past, when one steps cautiously out onto the rotted planks of such bridges as remain. She wasn't in the phone book, or hadn't been last time I'd looked, and I didn't know the name of the man she was living with, assuming she was still with him. Her parents had long since gone separate ways and sold their house; they were neither of them listed. What had become of Melanie? Had she enrolled in university? Written her book? Had she had another breakdown? Was it strange that she'd never tried to call me again – or had she perhaps left town? Suddenly I wanted badly to speak to her, to hear her voice again. I thought of her ebullience, her generosity of spirit. I remembered her screech of laughter that was pure delight. I imagined getting her number somehow, dialling it, astonishing her by singing "Happy Birthday" over the telephone – only, to give myself away, instead of "Dear Melanie" I'd sing "Dear Lemony," her baby name for herself and a childhood joke of ours. There would be a moment of shocked silence – then she would cry, "Is it Ruth? *No!* – is it *Ruth?*" – and I would hear that laugh. How nice it would be!

So she was on my mind when I got home from work and picked up my mail from the mat and read the postcard from Nora. And it was like – I can't say that I knew right then, that would be stretching it – but I knew there was something strange about getting that postcard on Melanie's birthday.

And later that evening, when I managed to connect (I remembered the name of a cousin of hers, I found him in the phone book, he was away on business but I spoke to his wife) – when I was told, hesitantly, that Melanie had passed away a couple of years back, she didn't want to say more, she'd have

Hal phone me when he got home next week . . . I didn't have to wait for the phone call. I knew right away, I felt in my stomach, the way she'd gone. The same way as Nora's friend. She'd hit the "DOWN" button – her way.

Hal phoned last night. He didn't remember me, but he remembered who I was. He remembered some of the games he and Melanie and I used to play in the courtyard behind the apartment building where he and she both lived as children, before Melanie moved to the suburbs: he even remembered the names of some of the kids from the building opposite, who used to play with us. We talked for a long time. It felt strange to talk to this grown man, married and with children of his own, virtually a stranger, and to find in his memory bank things I too remembered and things I had not remembered, which now flashed vividly before me. As a teenager Melanie had had something of a crush on him. She saw him infrequently, at family holiday gatherings, and she used to phone me afterwards to report: "Remember Harry, my cousin?" – he was Harry in those days – "Well, I saw him on the weekend and he's three inches taller than I am. He's even shaving. And you know what? He's gotten really cute!" They used to talk on the phone; one summer they were at the same camp, and Melanie came home bemoaning the fact that first cousins weren't allowed to marry.

"I always stayed in touch with her," Hal told me. "We spoke to each other pretty regularly, every two-three months anyway, right up until the end. Apart from the funeral I only met her boyfriend once – they came to my wedding. He seemed like an okay guy, but he didn't like to socialize, and it was hard for her to get out and around on her own. So mostly it was phone calls." He admitted it was usually Melanie who did the calling.

"You know, she always had her problems," he went on. "You must know that. I think she may have been manic-depressive, she was on pills, I don't know what exactly. But it went way back. Even at camp – she was always in the infirmary, she couldn't keep food down. They called it nerves. Why she did what she did – why at that moment – who can say? Apparently things were going all right, there wasn't any crisis, she was getting along fine with Stevie. She was even going to school – taking courses in English literature, I think, something like that. Getting A's. Figure it out. You know she'd tried before, though, you did know that, didn't you? In her early twenties."

"I thought she had an accident," I heard myself saying. "She told me it was an accident. That she fell off a fire escape."

"No, no. It wasn't an accident. It was the same thing – off a building – but only three storeys that time. She told you it was an accident?" And down tumbled my loving invention: the sun streaming into the little kitchen, the flowerpots on the fire escape, the vivid vermilion of the oranges in their purple tissue. Paula; the cats. Had I ever really believed it?

Not an accident.

He filled me in briefly on the family, the funeral, Melanie's parents. In the background I could hear small children tussling and squalling; he interrupted himself a couple of times, "Jonathan, put it down. I said PUT IT DOWN. Tracey, let go of his leg. Go brush your teeth – did you do pooh yet?" The third time, he laughed apologetically and said, "Listen, things are sort of degenerating around here, my wife's out at a daycare meeting. Can I give you my aunt's address, in case you want to write to her? You can call me anytime if you want to talk more."

I took down the address. "Thanks, Hal."

"Yeah, well, thanks too. I'm sorry. I appreciate your calling. It's nice to know she's remembered."

As soon as I put the receiver down, Bronwen marched in. "Are you off now? Rachel was supposed to *phone* me, we have to arrange stuff for tomorrow, *I* can't call *her* 'cause she's at her grandmother's and I don't have the number. How's she supposed to phone me if you're on the phone the whole night?"

"Don't whine. What's tomorrow?"

"Mom, I told you a million *times*, Rachel and Jessica and I have to get together to finish our geography project, it's due Monday, we have like *two days*!"

"Why'd you leave it so late, then?" Caitlin, in her prissiest voice. "I'm sorry, but I'm calling Rosemary back, she phoned while we were eating dinner and I promised."

"*Mom*! You can't let her!"

They're eleven and twelve now, in a year Caitlin will be the age Melanie was when she wanted to marry her cousin. She's going to camp for three weeks this summer; Bronwen went last. Even with Murray's contribution and help from parents, I can't afford to send them both in one year. I try to imagine Caitlin in the infirmary, throwing up, but I can't: Caitlin has a cast iron stomach. It's Bronwen I sometimes worry about, Bronwen who's high-strung, moody, who gets sent home from school with unexplained stomach pains or who wakes in the night with violent headaches – Bronwen for whom I leave work early or call in late, fuming over lost pay and unbudgeted taxi fares and three-hour waits in clinic waiting rooms to be told, "She's okay, we can't find a thing." Yet it's Caitlin whose teachers say, year after year, "We worry about her sometimes, her work is lovely but she seems so rigid somehow, so very self-controlled, we never see her let go and just have fun like the other children." I wonder what they used to say to Melanie's mother – the doctors, the teachers. I wonder what they didn't say.

September sunlight is streaming down through the tall schoolroom windows: long, slanted afternoon beams in which the dust motes circulate dreamily, just out of reach. It's the first day of second grade, five-past-three, time to go home. To our class has fallen the teacher everyone says is the best, the one everyone has had their fingers crossed to get: Miss Carsley, the pretty, smiling teacher everyone adores. In the schoolyard this morning they told us we were lucky ducks: "You have Miss Carsley? Oh, you lucky duck!" But lovely Miss Carsley has just betrayed us, has stunned us, by saying she will keep the entire class after school until the person who whistled in the cloakroom "owns up." It's deathly quiet in the classroom. The bell has rung; the staggered footsteps of class after dismissed class have receded down the corridors; only we are left. We are sitting in our seats with our sweaters or jackets on and our school-bags packed and our hands folded on our desks, waiting.

And nobody owns up. The red hand on the big classroom clock jerks away the seconds. Somebody shuffles and fidgets, somebody else coughs. "I can wait all night, if necessary," says Miss Carsley, her lovely features unperturbed, seating herself at her own desk and beginning to sort through some papers, just as though we were no concern of hers at all. Oh! the wickedness; she can't really mean it! Our eyes are upon her, wide with dismay.

Maybe five minutes have passed this way, but it feels like hours. I have my hand raised, but Miss Carsley doesn't look up. Without my consent, humiliatingly, something like a sob escapes me; at this she responds. "Yes, Ruth, what is the trouble?"

"My grandmother will worry if I'm late," I relay this plea shakily. My grandmother is babysitting today. Once last year, when I dawdled after school to play in a puddle, she called the police.

Across the aisle and two seats down, a dark-haired girl in a yellow sweater has raised her hand too.

"I have to meet my mother," she explains. "It's to go shopping. If I'm late she'll think I forgot and went home!" At the end her voice breaks too, she sniffs back tears. There's an undercurrent of derisive snorting from the boys.

"That will stop now," says Miss Carsley. "It so happens that I *know* who whistled, but I'm waiting for him to say so himself. For every five minutes that he delays the class, he can stay an extra ten."

The culprit capitulates. The rest of us are released. Standing on the corner, waiting for the crossing guard, I find myself next to the girl in the yellow sweater – the other girl who cried. We look at each other covertly; tentatively, we smile. Ordinarily aloof with new children, I feel bold with this girl who has revealed in herself a fragility equal to mine. I ask her name.

"Melanie," she says shyly, and then, smiling, suddenly eager to share: "When I was little, I couldn't say it. I said Lemony. What's yours?"

We both hated cooked carrots, arithmetic, skipping-rope games. We both got carsick. We were both obedient with teachers, timid with storekeepers, judgmental of our peers. We were always in the most advanced reading group. At recess we seldom joined the other girls; we had our own games, they were more fun. They were continuing fantasies, sagas, in which we starred in various roles, seizing upon whatever we had recently read or learnt, and whatever the season had to offer in the way of props and landscape: fallen leaves and candy-wrappers through the windy days of fall; snow mountains in winter, in whose caves we mined and cached ice diamonds, and down whose slopes we rolled giant round snow cheeses; canals, and lakes with icebergs, and glaciers of slush, during spring melting.

Early on, she confided to me, "I have a thing I do, I always wonder if everyone does it. I call it the 'She' game. It's when I'm by myself, like walking home from school or something, or even when I'm home, I'm always thinking the story of what I'm doing, and sometimes I even say it out loud, like: *She trudged wearily up the stairs*, or *She raced into her room and flung herself down on the bed.* Do you ever do that?" I did do that. I was astonished and pleased to learn that somebody else did. When we played together at recess, as it developed, we played a variant of the "She" game; we played the "They" game. We narrated our adventures in turn, generous with each other, acting it out as we went along. Eagerly taking each other's cues, we invented other lives, ones we lived in tandem with our real lives. When she moved away, a bleakness fell over the schoolyard, and recess dragged. I tried to continue the stories by myself, but it wasn't the same.

I can remember when my girls were little, waking early on weekend mornings and hearing them in the next room, narrating an accompaniment to their own play. It was that same endlessly inventive give-and-take, like jazz improvisation – Caitlin taking the lead and Bronwen jumping in, elaborating, embellishing. How it would pick up energy like a kite taking off, how they'd begin to interrupt each other excitedly, "No, Bronwen; Bronwen! listen to me; I have a better idea, it *wasn't* a camper van, it was a *covered wagon!*" "Murray," I'd whisper, gently joggling him awake. "Murray. Listen!" And we would tune in briefly, smiling into each other's sleepy eyes, tickled by their urgent pitch, their earnest baby voices. Then we'd doze off again, fading luxuriously in and out of sleep for as long as the game lasted before somebody fell and hurt herself or somebody got hungry; or till one of them, tiring of the play, sabotaged it into a squabble, and the grownup day began.

In those days I still thought Murray and I could make it work. I still thought that what we'd done together, what I'd persuaded him to do ("They married and moved to the west coast and started a family") was a story we could both keep adding to comfortably, a story we could both go with to last our lives.

So many holes, so many missing pieces. I'm looking back now, from a great distance, at those two little girls – not *my* two little girls (grown suddenly, bewilderingly, as tall as I am, borrowing my clothes without asking) – but the two who cried on the first day of second grade and became best friends. I see them in the spring, standing on the edge of an immense puddle in the schoolyard, looking down: the water is very still, a black mirror reflecting a still-bare tree, overhanging branches, beyond them a few clouds moving slowly across blue sky. "Stand right here," Melanie is saying, "and I'll show you something strange. No, don't lean over, you have to stand where you don't see yourself – just the sky. And there can't be any sun on the water. And there can't be a wind, it won't work if there's ripples. Now – look at the branches and then look past them at the clouds. *Stare*, I mean. Don't blink. There – are you starting to feel it? Do you feel like you're going to fall *down* into the sky? Like it's pulling you in? Isn't that scary?" They both feel it; they teeter for balance, laughing, and grab for each other. What would it be like to fall *down* into the sky? The teacher has been reading *Alice in Wonderland* to the class; would it be like Alice falling down the rabbit-hole – falling and falling and falling, but slowly, with time to think and look around? Would you keep falling forever?

And I see them in the summer, at Belmont Park where Melanie's mother has taken them for Melanie's birthday; they're trying to figure out how it is that when you get to the top of the Ferris wheel, your seat isn't upside down; they can't figure it out but Melanie has been on the Ferris wheel before and promises that it isn't. "You'll see, Ruth, it's the *most* fun. The best part is where you're right on top and it stops. And you can see everything far away, and everything on the ground is so tiny – everything looks *toy*. It's a little scary but not *very* scary. Like thinking it might get stuck and you couldn't get down. But when you look all around – well, you'll see – it's wonderful! You kind of wish things could just stay that way – the way it looks from up there."

I see them at the top of the Ferris wheel, tiny, gesturing against the sky. They have cones of cotton candy, beautiful pink, that Melanie says are like eating air.

If you were to say that as a child she had an attraction to the idea of heights, to the idea of falling – would you have explained anything? If you remembered that she had a terror of the skylight shaft off the bathroom of the apartment where she lived when you first knew her – would it be a clue? Does it mean more to say a word like *manic-depressive*? To ask if there had been a crisis, if there had been a quarrel?

"Ruth," I hear her saying, we're standing outside her door on the fourth floor landing, we're seven years old, "Do you know what a skylight is? Because there's a skylight in my bathroom."

It's the first time I've been to her house. I don't know what a skylight is, I live in a duplex. Melanie's building is a squat, ugly five-storey apartment house, dun-coloured brick – one of so many identical postwar buildings, both sides and the length of her block, that it takes months before I recognize which is hers as we approach it. Melanie has made her announcement as if she were saying, "There's a monster in my bathroom," and now she asks, worriedly, "Will you be afraid to use the bathroom?" She's hoping I can sleep over.

The skylight, I soon see, is just a narrow shaft the window gives on, a dim brick well down which faint daylight filters, yellowish, through dirty panes. Windows give on it on all four sides. Across from Melanie's, someone has put a plant out on the sill. "What's at the bottom?" I ask.

Melanie shrugs. She's standing in the doorway, watching me. "You can look if you stand up on the toilet seat and lean your head against the screen. I looked once. It was just some old mops and brooms. I don't know why it scares me. My mother made me look so I'd stop being scared, but I still am. I never close the door when I'm in there."

What in us cries out for an explanation? Why can I not just say, "My childhood friend grew up to suffer from a mental illness that led to her suicide in her mid-thirties"? For surely that is the essence of what happened to Melanie – as much as is given us to grasp. What is it exactly that one wants explained? The act? The timing? The method? "Why her?" The implications for oneself?

All of it, bewildering – impossible to accept – too painful to think about. I jump away from it – as I must have jumped away from my own suspicions, other people's intimations, about the "accident." No, no, it couldn't have been that; I believed Melanie. I preferred to believe what Melanie told me, to accept her story. More than that: to re-create it from the cues she gave me – to embellish it, add on to it, *make* it be real. Did I invent Paula to be for Melanie what I knew inside I had not been? Someone whose door was open to her, who didn't back away. Someone who needed her.

After the girls fell asleep last night, I went downstairs – I went down to the basement and, for the second time this week, opened the old steamer trunk under the stairs. The trunk is an antique; I bought it in a junk shop in Victoria, as a pretty thing to store linens in, and used it to ship the shards of my life back east in when I split with Murray. Once here, I unpacked what was useful and banged the lid down on everything else, all the old pictures and papers and memorabilia that had crossed the continent with me, some of it twice. Things that had become obsolete, like my half-written master's thesis and the notes for

it, maternity clothes, baby clothes – and things I couldn't bear
to look at, like wedding pictures and baby pictures and family
snaps. After we were legally divorced, I sifted through most of
it again and threw out a bunch of stuff, had a few of the old pictures framed, pulled out some odds and ends that had decora-
tive or sentimental value, and re-packed what was left. Since
then I seldom lift the lid, except at the end of each December
when my used-up calendar gets added to the pile, and whatever
letters I've kept over the year are filed away.

When I opened it last night, the calendar from the year
Melanie died was still on top where I left it last week. That
wasn't what I was after; I wanted to see if among my childhood
relics buried at the bottom, there wasn't a picture, a letter, a
keepsake – some concrete reminder of my friend. In a brown
envelope labelled "Grade School" I found our third-grade class
picture, but to my disappointment Melanie wasn't in it; she
must have been absent the day it was taken. I dug around
for a while thinking there might be something else, maybe a
snapshot of us at Belmont Park or at some other birthday celebration, maybe an autograph book, a card . . . but there was
nothing. And then, as usually happens when I dip into the
trunk, I sat leaning against its ribbed side on the cool basement
floor for a long time, diverted by what I'd pulled out to get at
what I was looking for – poking into things and reading things
before I put them back. I found a packet of old letters Murray
wrote me from the coast during the summer we were apart, a
year after we met. It was strange to read them again (I'd forgotten they existed) and to see, in retrospect, how clear it was from
their tone – coolly intellectual, controlled, enjoying their own
cleverness – that he was not much in love with me, that these
were not love letters. Yet I remember receiving them, I remember tearing them open sitting on the front stairs of the rooming-
house where I then lived, and reading love into them, because
it was what I'd decided was happening, because it was what I
wanted.

The thing I wish I'd kept to remember Melanie by – and it
was something I did keep for a long time, I still had it knocking

around my room when I was in high school – was a cut-glass doorknob that Melanie spotted on the way home from school with me one day, in a rubble heap from a building where there had been a fire. This became for the two of us something of a sacred object, central to much of our play, where it figured at one time as a fabulous jewel we had to protect against thieves or recover from thieves, at another as a talisman of magical powers, but oftenest as a divining crystal, a crystal ball. We took turns keeping it in our houses; I forget how it ended up with me – probably that's just where it happened to be when Melanie moved. Its facets caught and flashed the light, reflecting distortions of nearby objects, and we liked to gaze into it and describe to each other the worlds we saw inside, imagining ways we could make ourselves small and enter them. That was an idea Melanie came back and back to; when our teacher finished *Alice in Wonderland* and followed with *Through the Looking Glass*, she was enthralled – "Ruth," she used to say, "don't you *love* the part where the mirror begins to get hazy and she climbs through, into a different world? Don't you wish we could do that? Sometimes when I'm alone in the house I stand in front of the big mirror in the hall and stare and stare at it, and just *wish* it would happen. And once I thought it *was* getting hazy, but it was just my eyes, from staring."

It was well after midnight when I came back upstairs, checking on the girls before turning in as I always do. It's warm these nights; their window was open and the curtain was bellying in the breeze, lilac fragrance wafting in. An invisible line divides their room down the centre, Caitlin's side austerely tidy, Bronwen's looking as though a hurricane struck it; Bronwen's bed is closest to the door, and I caught my foot in a loop of her schoolbag strap, going in.

I like to look at them asleep; the years seem to drain from their faces and I see the pure lines of their features as I remember them from infancy. Caitlin's head was thrown back, hands clasped behind it, mouth open; her fine light hair was beginning to unravel from the elegant French braid her friend

Rosemary did up for her earlier this week. Bronwen lay on her stomach, arms around the pillow as though she'd fallen asleep tackling it. Her forehead was jammed against Digory, a plush dog she's had since she was five or six and still sleeps with, unabashed. Caitlin used to have a bedful of stuffed animals, but retired them to the closet a couple of years ago; Bronwen, whose fierce loyalty to Digory has precluded any other stuffed toy's joining him by her pillow, shows no signs of following suit; it was a foregone conclusion that he'd go to camp with her last summer.

I moved Digory away a few inches and lifted the hair from Bronwen's forehead, which was damp beneath my hand. She stirred in her sleep, a childish, sensuous movement, and renewed her hold on the pillow; she sighed. Digory slid to the floor and as I bent to retrieve him, I remembered another stuffed dog, I remembered the sad true story of Jackadandy, as told to me in the schoolyard by Melanie, not long after we first became friends. Jackadandy was her oldest toy, she'd had him from when she was still a baby; he was greyish and threadbare from going through the wash, and his legs had gone floppy so he couldn't stand up anymore, but he was still her Jackadandy. By a terrible mistake, Jackadandy had got thrown out with the garbage one day. Melanie had been playing Space Dog with him, she'd made him a space suit out of a brown paper bag, and stuck him in her wastebasket for a Sputnik capsule, and had forgotten and left him there. When she remembered, she found that her wastebasket had been emptied that morning. Her mother hadn't looked, she thought it was just an old lunch bag in there. And the big garbage had been emptied too, because it was garbage day.

"We ran outside right away," Melanie said. "We went around the side of the building where all the garbage is put out, but we were too late – the garbage truck had already been. So I asked my mother where the garbage trucks take the garbage – where does the garbage go? And she told me it goes down the river. So now," she concluded earnestly, touching my arm, "when I think of Jackadandy, I just tell myself, 'Jackadandy went down the river.' And that way, I can imagine all the adventures he must be having." She paused, she searched my face, did I understand? "Instead of feeling sad."

I guess it was something of the sort that I was casting for, down in the basement, when I sat on the floor with the letters in my lap and the picture in my hand, wishing that I'd kept the doorknob. It was crazy, but I guess I thought that if only I had the doorknob, the crystal doorknob – maybe I could look inside it and see Melanie, restored to wholeness, safely passed through.

In memoriam
E.M.S.

VIVIAN PAYNE

Free Falls

I t started out to be another quiet day in the diner. The weather was cold and bright, the cars crunched snow under their tires, and, inside, the windows steamed up from the moist heat generated by the kettles and the grill.

Helen was on the counter, taking orders and re-filling coffees. Even at this early hour, her make-up was impeccable and her hair was perfectly arranged in a neat, if somewhat anachronistic, roll. This was how Helen had appeared every day since she had arrived one morning several years ago applying for the advertised waitressing job. Even now, no one knew much about Helen other than that she worked in the diner and that she was nice. Where she came from and what her life had been before was not known. Not that she was dishonest; if there'd been a section on the application form asking for such details, she'd probably have filled it out, but Ed, who owned the diner, deemed that sort of information unnecessary and a waste of his time to analyze, so the only information on the form was her name and address. Helen must have agreed with him because she didn't volunteer anything extra, then or since. She was just Helen. She opened the diner, her grooming was perfect, and her manner friendly. There wasn't a ripple on the smooth surface she presented every morning to the regular clientele.

"Helen, more coffee, honey. When ya gonna marry me? I got the hall booked." Roy's weekly proposal. He had a wife already and five kids to prove it.

"Next Tuesday, sweetie. Four o'clock," was Helen's good natured reply as she poured him another coffee.

"That's what ya said last week and I lost my deposit, girl, 'cuz you never showed up." He grinned around the room at Ike and Ed. They grinned back. They heard this every week. Roy only came in on Mondays; it was the morning Betty allowed him to have to himself. The other mornings he was responsible for cooking breakfast for the five kids. But Monday mornings were his and he came down to the diner. In absolute equity, Betty got Monday night off dinner. The only ones to complain about the arrangement were the kids. All Roy knew how to cook was porridge, so Monday-night dinner was just Monday breakfast ten hours late. Monday nights, Betty came to the diner and took her turn asking Ed to marry her.

"My hairdresser let me down. She went and cancelled my appointment. I couldn't get married with a rat's nest for a hairdo, now could I?"

"Honey, I'd marry you if you had a wasp's nest for a hairdo."

Ed stuck his head out of the cubbyhole cut into the wall that separated the customer service area from the kitchen. "Helen, quit flirtin' with the customers and pick up your orders. This bacon's petrifyin' on this plate."

Helen waltzed over to the cubbyhole and whisked the plate up and away. "That's right, Ed. Make it sound real delectable. Who ordered the petrified bacon? We got petrified bacon on special today." She shot him a grin, showing her teeth and crinkling her nose. He mimicked her, showing his teeth and crinkling his nose. He punctuated his grin by pitching a bun at her head. She ducked and it missed her, but it hit Ike's coffee cup, upsetting it and him.

"Hey," Ike exclaimed, "did I come here for coffee or foolishness?"

"Ya came here to wake up, you old bugger, and that seems to have done the trick, so quit bitchin'. Helen, don't charge him for that coffee. Give him another one, and charge him for that one."

"Gee, thanks, Ed," Ike replied as he mopped the counter

with his napkin. "Helen, if it wasn't for your smilin' face, I don't know why I'd bother with this place."

"Hey, she's my girl, ain't ya, Helen?" Roy looked around to get Helen's comeback, but Helen had moved over to the window and was looking out into the street with a puzzled expression. "Helen, you're my girl, right?"

"Right as rain, Roy." She moved away from the window with a sudden efficiency. She whipped a cloth out of the sink and briskly wiped her way all down the counter, lifting coffee cups and plates up and out of the way as she went. "Don't you men have nothin' to do but sit here and jaw all day? I got work to do."

Ed said, "Hey, I should have thought of throwing buns at her a long time ago."

Across the street, a fifteen-year-old Chrysler crunched to a stop by the curb. The rumpled and musty man driving the car got out, walked around it, and inspected his parking job. It was on a bit of an angle. He carefully analyzed the situation and decided that his rear was a little too exposed. He went back around the car, got in and tried again, this time with a little more success – enough success that he nodded with satisfaction after he walked all around it again. He methodically locked all the doors. That done, he straightened himself up, patted his pockets to make sure he had everything, and marched across the street to the diner. He remembered everything – where to go, what to say, what to do – everything, except to look both ways before crossing the street.

Minh Frijole MacPherson was a mail-order bride. She was not born in this country although she was very happy with it and with her lumberjack husband. He was gone eleven out of the twelve months of the year, and her mother back home assured her this was a blessing. So far she had borne five children, one for every one of the five years she had been in Canada, and all five coincidentally enough shared the same birthdate which coincidentally enough was exactly nine months from the first day of her husband's annual vacation. She liked her children, she liked her husband, she liked her new country, but she hated driving. Pregnant with her sixth child, she had had to learn to drive in order to get the first child, now five years going on six, to Canadian kindergarten. Other mothers might have made him walk, but Minh MacPherson wanted to be better than the other mothers. She made the supreme sacrifice and she taught herself how to drive so that she could deliver him safe, sound, and warm to Canadian kindergarten. On this particular morning, little five going on six Ha Hugh MacPherson had misplaced his mittens, causing a frantic search that resulted in their leaving ten minutes late. With all her children bundled in the car, Ha Hugh crumpled apologetically in the back seat, sitting on his mittened hands to hide their mittened shame, Minh MacPherson pulled around the corner onto the main street with uncharacteristic aggression and struck down a pedestrian. In confusion, with four children screaming, one sulking and one kicking in the belly, she stopped the car and put it into reverse, to back up and see what she had hit. She hit the man again in the process.

Minh fainted. Four of her children screamed and cried; Ha Hugh looked at his mittens in horror at what he had done. If only he had put them in his pocket last night as he was supposed to do. But he hadn't. And now look. He made Mama kill somebody. And worse, it kind of looked like Mama was dead too, the way she was slumped over the wheel. He lifted her eyelids and only saw the whites of her eyeballs. She'd said she'd learn to drive if it killed her, and it apparently had, and someone else too. He was the oldest and he made a decision. He would have to get his father. He climbed out of the car, told his brothers and sisters not to worry, and walked resolutely up the street.

In the diner, nobody noticed what was happening in the street until Ike got up to go to the bathroom. The toilet in Ed's Men's Room was frozen up and it was beneath Ike's dignity to use the Ladies, so he bundled up and went outside to use the washroom at the post office down the way. He saw Minh's car parked crazily in the street, shook his head at some people's notion of parking and hurried on to the post office. Ike had a bad habit of leaving doors open. Roy, clad only in three layers, was the first to feel the draft. He got up to close the door, swearing rather more on top of his breath than under it. He too noticed Minh's car. He shook his head much like Ike had; the whole town had suffered when Minh undertook to learn how to drive, but really he thought she almost had the hang of it by now. Just before he closed the door, he saw a flutter in the snowbank under Minh's rear bumper. First a flutter, then a foot, then a leg. As Roy watched in amazement, a veritable snowman arose from the pile, threw his snowy head back, and bellowed, "Goddamn you anyway, Helen!"

Roy turned and looked back inside the diner. Helen had been wiping down the same table for the last five minutes, ever since Ed had thrown the bun at her head and she had looked out the window. When the snowman's bellow rolled through the open door and down the floor to where she stood, it hit her like a bowling ball. She fell backwards into a chair, put her wiping cloth to her forehead, and said, "Jesus H. Christ."

Roy looked back to the street. The snowman shook his fist at the diner, shuffled off to his car, got in, and lurched away. Roy looked back inside. Helen gave him a blank look, dropped the cloth from her head, and asked, "Is he gone?"

Roy was about to nod his reply when it came screeching through the air for him, "He's gone!"

Actually, what Minh had screeched upon coming out of her faint and counting her children was, "Ha's gone!" She got out of the car and began digging frantically in the snowbank. Roy ran across the street and tried to reassure her, repeating over and over, "Yes, he's gone. It's all right. He's gone. It's okay. He's gone." What Minh heard was, "Yes, Ha's gone. It's all right. Ha's gone. It's okay. Ha's gone." Roy was confused. The more he tried to calm her down and tell her that the snowman was gone, the more upset she became. His impulse was to pick her up and carry her into the diner. She was a small woman, but she was also a very pregnant small woman and he had no idea where to grab. She raged and dug in the snow; Roy yelled as soothingly as he could and flapped his arms vaguely about her body. Finally she collapsed, sobbing, and, clutching his knees, said softly, "Ha's gone." Roy, pleased that she finally believed him, patted her on the head and said, "There, it's all right, he's gone." Minh's other children climbed out of the car and stood staring up the road.

Inside the diner, Helen locked herself in the Ladies and didn't come out for an hour until all the excitement died down. Then she marched straight out, took up her cloth like it was a weapon, shook it at Ed, and said, "You got something to say?"

"No, ma'am."

"Then quit looking at me like that."

Ed, and Ike, continued to stare as Helen went back to work.

A muttered "Goddamn men" was all they got for their curiosity. They exchanged glances. Ed considered throwing another bun at her for a bit of comic relief, but thought better of it as he observed her thoughtfully polishing a butcher knife. She had a faraway look and was thinking faraway thoughts as her hand moved slowly and deliberately up and down the blade. Slowly she raised it up, staring fixedly at it as if fascinated by its shine. Ed and Ike watched her raise it up and up and up. They held their breath. Helen moved the knife slowly through the air until it was in front of her face. They watched in horror as she slowly turned the knife and stared into its gleaming blade. She curled back her lips and, turning her head from side to side, checked her teeth. With a dainty baby fingernail she dug between her two front teeth and said, "Ed, when you gonna put a mirror in the Ladies?"

Roy drove Minh and her children home. Minh sat in silence. The children huddled in the back seat in silence. He pulled into their driveway and had to urge them all to movement. Minh finally reached for the door handle and woodenly waddled up the walkway to the front door. Her children followed like bundled-up ducklings. The oldest girl carried the baby. They disappeared, one by one, through the door into the house without a look back. Roy followed them in. Minh headed straight up the stairs without taking off her coat. The children went into the kitchen and sat in a row at the table, the baby at the end in a high chair. Each child sat in front of a dirty cereal bowl and a dirty juice glass. There was an extra dirty cereal bowl and an extra dirty juice glass. The three children stared at the empty chair in front of the empty place. The second youngest, the almost-two-year-old, started to cry. The baby threw his bowl and laughed. Roy counted the places and counted the children, and finally he understood.

After all his excitement in town, Harry pulled his fifteen-year-old car over to the side of the road just outside the town limits. He had an overpowering need to collect his thoughts and an overpowering need for some painkiller. He flipped open the glove compartment and fumbled until he found his emergency flask. He took a long pull, wiped his lips on his coat sleeve, and let his head fall back against the seat. He considered the success of his mission. He took another drink. At least he knew where she was. But then again, now she knew he knew where she was, so maybe she wouldn't stay put. And he'd have to start all over again. After all these years, he'd finally decided to see things her way and tracked her down to tell her so she'd come back. He was going to march right in there and tell her, declare his undying love, in front of strangers even; she'd like that, wouldn't she? Just like in those romantic novels she had hidden from him. He'd read them all after she left. At first he'd thought his insomnia was simply due to heartbreak, but then he found the novels stuffed under the mattress. "See," he'd said out loud when he found them, "I'm not insensitive at all. I'm a veritable princess with a pea." But Helen wasn't there to hear him. She was gone.

He took another swig. A movement on the road beside the car caught his eye. He turned his head and saw a small figure trudging resolutely along. The boy did not even turn his head to look at him. He just kept trudging along with his head down and his arms swinging at his sides. Harry rolled down the window.

"Hey, boy! Where you goin' with such a purpose?"

The boy ignored him and kept on trudging. Harry got out of the car and stepped after him. Ha heard the car door and the footsteps scuffling in the sand on top of the snow-covered road. He made another decision and broke into a run. Harry leaped ahead and grabbed him by the hood of his snowsuit.

"Whoa, there, boy." Harry lifted Ha in the air by the hood of his purple ski jacket. The boy hung loosely in his grasp but his look was grim, his lips pressed tight. Roy put him down.

"I am not a boy. I am a man," he stated flatly as Harry knelt down and straightened out his snowsuit. Ha allowed himself to be patted and pulled back into shape. When Harry was done, Ha did his own patting and pulling. When he had himself re-arranged to his own liking, he turned and started away again. Harry hesitated, then followed.

They walked along in silence for a minute. Ha, without turning his head, stated again, "I am not a boy. I am a man."

"I'm beginning to believe it, son. But you never answered my question. Where you goin' with such a purpose?"

"I must find my father."

"Did he go somewhere?"

Ha stopped and gave Harry a look that made Harry realize the stupidity of the question. He tried to apologize, "Obviously he went somewhere, but do you know where he went? That helps, you know."

"Up north."

"Up north? Where up north? There's lots of places up north."

"There are?" As far as he knew, his father walked out the door, got in the car, pulled out of the driveway, turned the cor-ner, and was then "up north." It wasn't very far away. Ha knew because one time he'd asked Mama where Father had gone right after Father had turned the corner and Mama had said "up north." "Up north" should have been right around the corner. But it wasn't. And now here was this man talking like it wasn't a particular place but something that contained a lot of places. He looked ahead on the road and all of a sudden he realized that it didn't seem to end anywhere, it kept going. He looked at the bush lining the road. It kept going too. In all directions. He was in the middle of something that didn't seem to be a particular place and didn't have any familiar edges. The world so far had been quite well defined by a creek on one side, a cemetery on another, the schoolyard fence, and Happy LaDing's Used Cars. Suddenly he felt very small and more five than six. Ha allowed a five-year-old's expression of fear to pass over his face. For the first time, he allowed to himself that he was just a child and that he was out on an endless road in an endless snowy bush without his mother.

"There are, little man."

"Which one is my father in?" Ha asked haltingly, holding back the sobs that were choking up his throat.

"I don't know, son." Harry put his hand down on the boy's shoulder. The touch on his shoulder broke Ha's pretence. Under the arm of an adult, he was only a small boy, and he threw his arms around Harry's waist, hung on tight, and cried, "Mama!" Harry cradled him up, stroked his back, patted his behind, and said, "There, there," as he carried Ha back to the car. "We're all lookin' for somebody."

Back in town, Roy strode into the diner.

"Helen, who was that man?"

Helen didn't spill a drop of the seventh cup of coffee she was pouring for Ike. Ike looked over at Ed. Things just kept on getting more and more interesting. "What man?"

"Helen, he took the kid."

Helen paused. "He wouldn't take a kid."

"Helen, Ha MacPherson is gone. That man, that abomination in the snowbank took him."

"The last thing that man wants is a kid." She went back to pouring Ike's coffee.

"Thought you didn't know him."

"I don't know him." She stood up straight with a vehemence that caused the coffee to splash out over the brim of the pot. Ike jumped back to avoid the splash. "Aww, Helen! Ed, she got me again, all over my good slacks."

"Don't worry, I won't charge you for it," Helen said flatly as she walked to the back of the diner. Roy followed her. Ike dabbed at his lap with a paper napkin. It shredded and made matters worse.

"Helen, this kind of behaviour is not like you. What's goin' on and where is that kid?"

Helen put down the coffee pot on the table outside the

Ladies and turned to face Roy. "He didn't want kids then, and he doesn't want any kids now." With that she slammed into the Ladies and locked the door.

Ed came out of the kitchen. "Jesus, Roy, she was in there for an hour last time, no telling how long you scared her into it now."

"But, Ed, the kid is missing."

"The kid is probably at school, where he's supposed to be. You check the school?"

"No."

"Then get your butt out of here and make sure you know what you're talkin' about before you terrorize my waitress into permanently barring the way to the only working toilet I got left."

Ike picked fragments of napkin out of his lap. "It seems our Helen has a past. Judging from the evidence." He rolled a shred between his fingers and flicked it in the air. "A colourful past."

"None of your goddamn business, you old bastard!" came the reply from behind the Ladies' door.

Roy turned and left. Ike was shocked. Helen had only ever treated him as a special and honoured guest. Old bastard? Is that what she really thought? He looked to Ed for an explanation. Ed shrugged his shoulders.

Lying on her bed, Minh felt a familiar twinge in her belly. She pulled the covers up and stubbornly denied it. She would not have her sixth child until her first one was returned to her. Downstairs in the kitchen, the children cleared away the breakfast dishes and then wondered what to do with themselves. They didn't feel like playing. 'Sesame Street' was on but they weren't allowed to touch the TV set. Mama had to turn it on, and she was up in bed. The three oldest crept up the stairs. The baby crawled after them. Yup, she was in bed, all right, with the covers pulled right up and a funny look on her face. They each took a stair and sat, chins in their hands, and waited. They wondered what Kermit was up to. They wondered what Mama was up to. They wondered what was going to happen next.

The front door opened and a young girl stuck her head in. "Hello?" They stared at her. They stared at her clothes. They stared at her hair. A teenager. A strange teenager.

"My dad sent me over."

This had no discernible effect on the four little statues perched at the top of the staircase, so Lisa Marie elaborated.

"My dad, Roy."

Still no effect.

"Where's your mother?" She took a step up toward them. They shrank back.

Four little fingers wavered upward and four sets of eyes pinned her to the spot.

"Sleeping?" She crept up another stair.

They had to consult on this. She was in bed but there was some disagreement about whether or not she was actually asleep. The boy on the very top stair ran to have a look. He came back and shook his head.

"Well, let's just leave her be. Like I said, my dad sent me to look after you for a while. What do you want to do? Isn't 'Sesame Street' on?"

Lisa Marie was almost knocked over in the rush down the stairs. The baby got kicked and started to cry. Lisa Marie picked him up and followed the crowd, with him resting on her hip. She came into the living room to find the three older children sitting expectantly in front of the television set. "I guess it is." She flicked the TV on and sat herself down on the couch. The baby pulled a barrette out of her hair and chewed it happily. Lisa sighed, well, things could be worse, her father could have made her go to school. A low and hurting moan came from the bedroom upstairs. The children, all except the baby who was now chewing on Lisa Marie's dangly earring, looked at the staircase and then at one another. "Say, is your mom sick or something?"

"She's having a baby."

"Now?"

Three small heads nodded. The baby grabbed her nose and laughed.

Harry pulled into the parking lot of a donut shop on the highway. Ha sat up in the passenger seat, pulled himself up by the dashboard, and balanced by pressing his forehead against the windshield. He turned his head from side to side, looking around and using his forehead as a pivot. "Now are we up north?" he asked in mingled hope and doubt.

"A little bit. I figure we ought to get something to eat and figure out a few things."

"I don't want to go home." Harry saw the little body stiffen within the soft and puffy contours of the purple snowsuit.

"I didn't ask you that, did I? I said we're going to get something to eat and figure out a few things, and that's what we're going to do." Harry got out of the car and walked across the parking lot. His easy-going gait showed the whole world, Ha included, that he had no concern for what Ha did. Ha could follow or not for all Harry appeared to care. In actual fact, he was straining his ears to hear Ha open the car door and follow. He heard the door open. He heard it close. He heard Ha's squeaking steps. He stopped and waited. By the time Ha caught up to him, he had arranged his face into a suitable semi-scowl.

"Okay, little man, tell me about yourself." Harry stirred the third packet of sugar into his coffee. Ha did the same. They both sipped. Ha made a face and Harry handed him another sugar packet. "What's your name? For starters."

"Ha."

"When?"

"Ha."

Harry practised it a few times till he got it to Ha's satisfaction.

"Is that an Inuit name?"

"It's a MacPherson name."

"Ha MacPherson, is that it? Glad to meet you, Mr. MacPherson." They shook hands. "I'm Harry Tullingbroke. And god only knows what kind of a name that is."

"It's a funny name."

"Thanks, kid, I needed you to tell me that. Now, what am I going to do with you?"

Ha poured another sugar into his coffee. "Can you take me to my father?"

Harry considered this. "Where's your mama?"

"Can I get a donut?" Ha squirmed around and eyed the donut counter, with one backward shift of his eyes to see if Harry had bought the change of topic.

Harry didn't. "Are they divorced or something? You running away from your mama?"

"Maple dip?" Ha said hopefully.

"I'll get you that donut if you tell me why you have to leave your mama. You shouldn't go leaving people that love you." Harry took a sip of his coffee and looked out into the parking lot as if he didn't care at all.

"I killed my mama." This was muttered into the purple snowsuit. Harry was pretty sure he'd heard it right but he wanted to be really sure he'd heard it right. He kept his eyes fixed on the parking lot, on the rear bumper of his car to be exact. He'd never noticed that dint before. "Did you say you killed your mother?"

"Yes."

Harry noticed every detail of the dint in that bumper. It seemed to have a little yellow paint on it, now that he looked closely, looked more like it had been hit than that it had done the hitting itself. He could only hope that the son of a bitch who'd hit his car had suffered more damage than he had. Paint was a good sign. That indicated that bodywork was in order.

"I want my father!" Ha collapsed on the table, spilling his coffee. "I hate my mitts, I hate my mitts!" He pulled them out of his pocket and threw them across the room, hitting the waitress who was cleaning the condiments table and causing her to drop the bottle of cheap ketchup she was using to re-fill the Heinz bottles. She turned and gave Harry a look that showed exactly what she thought of some people and their kids.

Great gasping groans rent the air. Minh rolled from side to side on the bed. Lisa Marie ran from side to side trying to make contact, trying to find out what to do. The children stared in through the doorway.

"Boil some water!" she shouted, and immediately wondered why. What would she do with it when she got it?

"We're not allowed to touch the stove."

"Call 911!"

"We're not allowed to touch the phone."

"Are you allowed to scream for help?"

They consulted. Not one of them had ever been forbidden yelling for help. Still they hesitated. You never knew, grown-ups had a way of making up the rules as they went. It wasn't until you went and did something that you found out you weren't allowed. That's how they'd found out about the stove and the phone. Suddenly, Mom screamed, "Help," herself, and that decided it. They ran down the stairs, jumping over the baby who was chewing contentedly on Lisa Marie's neon head-band. They ran outside, down the driveway and into the street, shouting, "Help!" all the way.

Betty came into the diner and stamped the snow off her boots. It was really coming down. "All right, where is she?"

Ed and Ike jerked their heads in the direction of the Ladies.

Betty hung her coat on the rack and rolled up her sleeves.

"Sure appreciate you comin' in like this, Betty," Ed said. "I think it needs a woman's touch."

"What's going on? Roy called and said she was hysterical. Said I had to get her out of the Ladies."

"We ain't heard a peep in an hour."

"Why's she locked herself up in there?"

Ed and Ike shrugged.

"Something must have happened. Somebody must have done something."

They shrugged again.

Betty knocked on the Ladies' door.

"Go away."

"Helen, it's me, Betty. I gotta go."

"The post office is just up the street."

"Helen, I gotta go now." Betty threw a special urgency into the word "now."

"Helen, now." There was a wheedle in Betty's voice. Helen considered opening the door, in her mind's eye she saw Betty squirming up and down as she squeezed her thighs together. "Helen, I got six kids, how much control do you think I got left? That post office might as well be in Siberia for how far it is."

Helen opened the door. Betty thanked her and went into the cubicle.

"My, this is a relief," Betty sighed.

"I'm not going to talk about it, so there's no point in asking me." Helen's tone was defiant.

"I just asked to use the bathroom. You didn't hear me asking for your life story, did you?"

"No." Helen had figured that Betty was here to get her out of the bathroom. She had worked up a righteous self-defence and now it seemed Betty didn't even want to hear it.

"You can lock yourself in here for life, long's you let me in when I need to get in." Betty's voice was almost cheerful. Helen began to get annoyed.

"You mean you don't want to know my life story."

"Maybe if you wrote a book, I'd read it, if it was good."

Betty flushed the toilet and came out of the cubicle straightening out her pantyhose. "God, I hate winter. These stupid boots twist my pantyhose all around. It's all that pile lining. Every step I take, the nap of that pile lining pulls the other way on my pantyhose and I end up so twisted up I have to walk sideways. Don't you hate that?"

"Yeah."

"Helen, you got a perfect life. You don't know it because I never told you, but I envy you. I do. You got a nice job, you got your own money, you got your own apartment without five kids playing music you don't understand, fighting over who used whose toothbrush to add texture to some plasticene project on the environment, coming in at all hours saying they were just over at Jeannie's, 'phone her Mom and ask, you don't really believe me.' But it's two o'clock in the morning, am I really gonna phone Jeannie's mom at two o'clock in the morning? I'm either gonna wake her up, find out somebody's lying, and then Jeannie's mom is gonna know my kid's a liar, or I'm gonna find out the kid was telling the truth and I'm gonna look like I'm a mean old bitch who doesn't trust her children. I'm telling you, you can't win with kids."

Helen sniffled.

Betty put her arms around Helen. "Oh, honey."

With the warmth of another body and the soft, dimpled strength of Betty's arms wrapped around her, Helen started to cry in earnest. Betty swayed back and forth ever so slightly, rocking Helen while she cried. "There, there," she crooned in long-practised sympathy. "There, there."

Back in the car and heading towards town, Harry was making little headway with Ha. "People just don't die like that. Did you hit your mother in the back of the head with a brick?"

Ha shook his head.

"Did you shoot her?"

Ha shook his head more forcefully.

"Did you strangle her with piano wire?"

"What's piano wire?"

"It's wire they use in pianos."

"What's a piano?"

"You've never seen a piano?"

"I saw a picture in a book."

It was Harry's turn to shake his head. "Kid, you've got a lot to learn. I told you you were still just a kid. I'm taking you back to your mama. She's not dead and you're gonna need to stick by her for a couple of years yet. Your dad'll find you when he wants to."

"But she is dead. I killed her."

"What did you do, smother her with those mitts you hate so much?"

Ha became indignant. "I lost my mittens."

"What are those things on your hands? Pancakes?"

Ha threw himself into a slump against the seat. He pulled his hood down over his eyes and his scarf up over his nose. "I found them," he growled through the wool as if Harry was just about the stupidest adult he'd ever run into.

"Can't hear you, kid. Your voice is kind of muffled."

Ha got angry. He turned in his seat, got tangled up in the seat belt, and after a brief struggle with that, he pulled his scarf down and shouted, "I found them! But I found them after a long time and I was late for school. Mama doesn't like it when I'm late for school, so she drove fast and she hit a man with the car. She killed him and then she died and I have to find my father up north because Mama is dead. I have brothers and sisters. It's my fault so I gotta find my father!" He crossed his arms as a silent "so there" and sat back in his seat, pulled his scarf back up, and stared straight ahead.

Harry kept driving. He made the turn towards town, pursed his lips, and made a sucking noise through his teeth, "Now we're getting somewhere."

Lisa Marie sat beside the phone and railed against the system. She had been taught when you're in trouble, phone 911. She'd phoned 911 and she'd been put on hold for what seemed like an hour. Minh was past the stage of rolling back and forth, she seemed to have settled into heaving and moaning. Lisa Marie was not sure if this was a good sign. When 911 finally came back to her, the voice on the other end was not very helpful. There were no ambulances in town, the nearest one would take over an hour to get there. If the lady was as far gone as Lisa Marie's information indicated, her best bet was to take her directly to the clinic in town. Lisa Marie hung up without bothering to inform 911 that she was only fourteen and her father, Mr. Be-Prepared-Area-Scoutmaster himself, had absolutely refused to teach her how to drive until she was sixteen. She could walk and ride her bike, get her exercise and grow strong bones, never mind her brothers had been driving since they were eleven. She phoned her father. He wasn't at work. Great. She phoned her mom. She wasn't at home. Even greater. Her brothers weren't at home. No doubt they were joy-riding around somewhere impressing ten-year-old girls. The injustices mounted. They better let her wear makeup after this. What to do? Another truly scary moan from Minh. Lisa Marie considered her options. She could try to drive Minh's car or she could deliver the baby. She thought about the video they'd shown in health class at school, "The Miracle of Birth." She decided it was time to learn how to drive. "They better let me wear blue eyeliner, screw the modest blush."

Helen and Betty had settled themselves on the bathroom floor, were smoking cigarettes and drinking the beer which Ed had obediently delivered when Betty stuck her head out the door and gave the order with the gravity of a physician prescribing a treatment for a serious illness.

"He couldn't say he loved me. I wanted to hear it and he just wouldn't say it. So I ran away." Helen took a swig and shrugged.

"You didn't run too far."

"I thought he'd come looking for me. I could have gone to the city. I should have gone to the city."

"But he has come looking for you."

"After three years. Three years."

"He came looking. Roy hasn't looked for me in sixteen years. Oh, I never ran away. I've been here, but he's never looked for me."

"But he loves you. He says so all the time."

"To you maybe. I only hear about how fond he is of his new rototiller."

"Harry didn't take that kid. I know Harry. Three years and I still know him. He don't want no kids. Kids are part of love, and Harry can't do love."

Outside in the diner, Roy and Lester arrived. Lester was the head of the volunteer fire department and the most official person Roy could find on short notice. The principal was on standby at the school. Roy exchanged meaningful glances with Ed and Ike. Ed poured the coffee. Roy jerked his head back towards the Ladies, his eyebrows raised significantly. Ed made the yakking gesture with his hands. Ike nudged Roy, and significantly raising his eyebrows higher than Roy's, mimed smoking cigarettes and tilting back beers. Roy's eyebrows lifted even higher than Ed's or Ike's. Women. Serious stuff to be done and what were they doing? Holed up in a washroom drinking and smoking and yakking. He shook his head at the sorry situation.

"Just waiting here for the RCMP, Ed. They're on their way."

Lester wiped the sleep out of his eyes and asked what the breakfast special was.

It got to be about that time for Ike. He got up and hauled his coat down from the rack in preparation for the long cold walk up to the post office. "Don't nobody do nothing till I get back. I don't want to miss nothing." He buttoned his coat with creaky fingers. Everyone watched as he pushed the second button from the top into the first hole from the top. With great dignity, he pulled his toque down over his ears and shuffled out.

Harry and Ha pulled up to the curb, or as close as they could get to it, considering the street hadn't been plowed and the amount of snow that had fallen in the last two hours.

"Look, kid, it was me your mama hit."

Ha sat still.

"It was."

Ha stared straight ahead.

"I'm not dead so she's probably not dead. It wasn't that violent an impact. Yeah, sure, enough to bruise me up a little."

Ha sat even more still.

"See? Look, here's a bruise." Harry's fingers scrambled to dig through layers of clothing. He succeeded and triumphantly displayed a purply spot spread over the roll of fat on the top of his hip.

Ha allowed his curiosity to get the better of him. He looked.

"Progress!" Harry thought, and exuberantly jumped out of the car. "Look, I'll show you!" He ran around to the back of the car. Ha turned in his seat to watch.

"See, I was just standing here like this. Remember?"

Ha began to recognize Harry now that he saw him in the context of the street and the snowbanks. He nodded.

"I was trying to gear myself up to go over into the diner there," he pointed across the street. "My wife is in that diner, and I never told her I loved her." He froze with his arm stuck in the air, the door of the diner was opening. He held his breath. This was just as he had imagined it all those nights alone. He'd be in the street, declaring his love, she'd look through the window, forget the coffee she was pouring and be drawn outside, pulled by the power of love, their love. Her steps would be slow at first, hesitant, but gradually they'd become firm and definite, building into surefooted haste as she ran across the street to fling herself into his open arms. Just like in those romance novels she had hid under the mattress. The door of the diner continued to open. It fully opened, Harry closed his eyes. He opened his eyes, with his arms widespread and his fingers crossed, and behold! An old man with a funny toque pulled over his ears and his coat buttoned up wrong. Harry dropped his arms. He looked back at Ha and shrugged sheepishly.

Minh hung on with both hands to the dashboard, her head down, her bursting body lurching, side to side and back and forth, as Lisa Marie experimented with the steering wheel, the gas pedal, and the brake. Three little bodies lurched about obediently in the back seat, a fourth stood, clutching Lisa Marie's headrest for dear life. With Daddy gone, and Ha gone, Mama in the throes of labour, four-year-old Nhan Alicia MacPherson knew her duty and she screeched helpfully into Lisa Marie's left ear. They slid around the corner onto the main street.

Stepping out into the cold, Ike felt a telltale draft. He stopped and examined his buttoning job. Finding it less than accurate, he began to make the necessary adjustment, which meant unbuttoning all the way down and then buttoning all the way up. He rolled his head in exasperation. The panorama that passed in front of his eyes as a result of this action included snow-covered sidewalks, snow-laden awnings, the snow-filled sky, and a rumpled, battered figure, standing with arms uplifted in joyful expectation. Ike's eyes met Harry's. Harry's arms fell. "Same to you, bud," Ike thought. He squinted at the rumpled and battered car that matched the rumpled and battered man.

The wonder of it all dawned on Ha when he saw Harry standing in the street. Nobody was dead. Mama must be somewhere. He didn't have to run away to find his father. Mama must be somewhere, maybe at home, no wait, wasn't that her car coming around the corner? Why was she going so fast? Why did she have blonde hair? Why did she have two heads? Why didn't she put on the brakes?

"Actually, we named her after Elvis' airplane." Betty was trying on some of the makeup Helen kept in the cupboard under the sink. She checked her eyeliner job in her fuzzy reflection on the brushed aluminum of the towel dispenser. "Why doesn't Ed put a mirror in here?"

"I was named after Helen of Troy." Helen stayed slumped on the floor.

Ike exploded through the doorway into the restaurant. "It's him! He's here! He's back!" Roy and Lester leapt into action, scrambling for their coats and their mitts.

Betty stopped mid-lipstick. Helen held her breath.

Harry froze, not believing that it was happening again. He'd come here to demonstrate the original incident, sure, but he'd been thinking more in descriptive and figurative terms than in literal.

Lisa Marie screamed, and her foot hit the gas instead of the brake. Nhan flew backwards into the laps of her various siblings. Minh, oblivious to all but what was happening low in her gut, uttered a deep and final moan. Ha jumped up and down inside Harry's car.

Harry bounced off the bumper of Minh's car and took his second unscheduled flight of the day into the snow piled at the side of the street.

The soft thudding of his body shuddered through the diner, all the way back to the Ladies.

"Harry!" Helen shoved Betty aside, fumbled with the latches on the door, threw it open, almost throwing it off its hinges. She pelted down the diner to the door. Roy, Ike and Lester were clutched at the door, blocking her way. They were still trying to figure out what they'd just witnessed. She pushed her way through their confusion.

"Harry?" Helen called.

"Daddy?" Lisa Marie called.

"Mama?" Ha called.

"Helen?" Harry called.

"Roy?" Betty called.

"Ha?" Minh called.

"Police?" Roy called.

"Doctor!" Nhan Alicia called. The only sane voice in the crowd.

Helen ran and fell on her knees beside Harry, who was

stretched out flat on his back in the middle of the snow-covered street, his head cradled in the groove of a tire track. He gazed up at the sky just as if he had lain down there on purpose to get the best possible view of it. It started to snow again, and a few large flakes settled on his nose. He didn't even twitch. He accepted them as the street itself accepted them.

"Harry, are you all right?"

No answer, just that unwavering stare at the sky. Helen hoped he wasn't staring into the Great Beyond. She went to shake him, but stopped suddenly when she thought she saw a slight tightening around his lips. Roy, Betty, Ed, and Ike came up behind her, slowly and noiselessly, with hesitating feet like cats approaching an unfamiliar object. They stared down at Harry over Helen's head.

Harry had a hard time keeping a straight face. "Helen...," he moaned piteously.

"Yes, Harry?" Helen replied carefully, not quite suspiciously, but she drew back a few inches anyway.

"Helen...," this was a whisper. Then he seemed to lose his strength, he closed his eyes and winced ever so slightly. His lips moved wordlessly. Helen leaned in. Roy, Betty, Ed, and Ike leaned down and in. His lashes fluttered, his eyes opened. Helen saw the pleading in them, and she leaned down. "Yes, Harry?"

"Told you you'd come running to me some day."

"Son of a bitch." She jumped up and threw a tantrum, flailing her arms, stamping her feet, and yelling, "Son of a bitch!" Roy, Betty, Ed, and Ike scattered. The snowflakes scattered. She started kicking the snowbank. Harry lay still and grinned because now he knew for sure she still loved him.

Roy was watching Helen in mute fascinated horror. He'd never seen Helen lose her cool. He'd never seen any woman lose her cool, Betty was the model of calm, even when extremely angry like the time he'd forgotten her birthday because he'd just gotten the new rototiller for the vegetable garden. She didn't throw a tantrum, she didn't say a word. She even volunteered to take care of the planting. It wasn't until he went to do some weeding a month later and noticed that the entire garden had been planted with zucchini that he began to think maybe he had annoyed her somehow. The day of the harvest, she presented him with a zucchini birthday cake with "Happy Birthday Betty" scrolled on top. That was when he remembered her birthday. He ate some cake. The next morning she chopped the rest of it up and mixed it with his bran flakes. He ate that too. He ate zucchini everything for a full month. Betty got him good, but she never yelled, and she never made a spectacle.

Betty too was watching Helen with fascination. But hers was rather more admiring.

Ed and Ike had taken refuge near Minh's car. They were watching with fascination too, but they weren't looking at Helen. The object of their attention was stretched out on the front seat giving birth to the newest MacPherson, with the able assistance of Lisa Marie, who was grateful she'd seen that video. It was turning out to be a lot more useful than any of those know-it-all adults.

Ha had climbed in the driver's door. He held his mother's head, stroking her hair and saying, "There, there." Minh was torn between paying attention to what was happening to her on the passenger side and her desire to rejoice over the sight of her firstborn, miraculously restored to her in her time of need.

Helen was just winding down when Roy felt a small tug on the sleeve of his ski jacket. He looked down and saw Nhan staring up at him as if she wanted him to do something. She let go and waddled towards the car. He followed.

"Sweet God Jesus! Betty, get over here!"

Minh was sitting up in the front seat of her car, with Ed's coat around her shoulders and Ike's coat bundled around her new baby girl, Lisa Kin Marie MacPherson.

Ike and Ed stood in their shirtsleeves, too busy grinning like idiots to shiver. Ha was organizing his brothers and sisters for a proper introduction to their new sister, pulling their coats this way and that, counting their mittens, and patting their hair into presentability. Lisa Marie gave Roy a dirty look and flipped herself into the snowbank. "Blue mascara, black eyeliner, red lipstick, and the car on Friday night." She crossed her arms decisively and stared at him with an "I dare you" in her eye.

Helen, too, had ended up in the snowbank, but she hadn't so much flopped into it as she had collapsed into it. Harry still hadn't moved. He waited until he was sure she was quiet. His face was almost completely buried by the fallen snow. He took a deep breath and blew to clear his mouth. A splutter of snow heralded the words that Helen had never before heard, "I love you."

JIM REIL

Dry

Two weeks after he got out of a Calgary treatment centre, Charlie was packing to go back to Toronto.

"You'd be better off with a couple months of sobriety under your belt," his AA sponsor said as Charlie stuffed socks and underwear into a scarred, black leather suitcase. Frank had been in the centre himself, three times. He was tall and painfully thin and had a slight stoop that got worse when he was tired.

Charlie sat on a half-filled cardboard box and wiped sweat from his forehead. "I've blown three contracts here, Frank. Who the hell would hire me?"

"Can you get work in Toronto?"

"To tell you the truth, I don't remember much of my last few months there. But you can bet Nancy will tell me all about it."

"When was the last time you spoke to her?"

Charlie lit a cigarette, grimacing as he inhaled. "Six months ago. She told me she'd get an unlisted number if I called again."

Although Charlie had lived in the apartment for eight months, he owned only two unmatched wooden chairs and an unsteady card table, plus a stained mattress he had dragged up from the basement. The living room walls were bare, but in the bathroom he had tacked up a tattered National Geographic world map salvaged from a cupboard.

When his few clothes were packed, Charlie heated up a can of tomato soup and put two chipped bowls on the card table. He was having difficulty keeping solid food down – his stomach churned constantly. He worried about ulcers, which had killed his father.

The soup tasted chalky and gritty to Charlie, but so did most things – for months now he'd been smoking more than two packs a day. Several ashtrays brimming with butts were stacked beside the sink.

Charlie pushed his soup aside and lit another cigarette. "It must be hard being around a heavy smoker," he said to Frank, who had finally quit a year ago.

"It's just like the booze," Frank said. "When you see someone still smoking heavy, you remember why you quit."

Charlie was giving the reeking toilet bowl a desultory scrub when the landlord buzzed from the lobby to be let up. Charlie had phoned Mr. Grunner from the centre, but when the old man began to scream in German, Charlie had hung up. Once Mr. Grunner had been enraged when the police refused to take Charlie to a psychiatric ward. Charlie had been drunkenly gracious to the two young police officers, and remembered feeling gloriously cunning.

Now when Charlie answered Mr. Grunner's brisk knock the landlord stood hunched and scowling in the dim hall. He was gaunt, his face harsh as February mornings. He wore suits that were too large and he had a drab, sour odour, like boiled cabbage. According to the building's plumber, who sneered as he told Charlie this, Mr. Grunner had made his fortune renting out tenements in Berlin after the war.

"When are you leaving?" Mr. Grunner demanded.

Charlie shook his head. "We've been through this a dozen times."

Frank came to the door. "This is the landlord," Charlie said. "He thinks I'm trying to shaft him."

"You're not a good tenant," Mr. Grunner muttered.

"What's the problem?" Frank asked.

"It's a long story, but I've paid the rent for this month."

Mr. Grunner pushed past Charlie. "I look around," he said, shuffling into the empty living room where his heavy shoes scraped loudly across the hardwood floor. Charlie followed Mr. Grunner, imagining the old man wandering through the ruins of some bombed-out Berlin tenement, kicking shards of glass across the floor. Mr. Grunner was in his eighties, and why should he trust anyone? He certainly didn't expect anyone to trust *him*.

"What is this?" he demanded, pointing to a brown stain spilling down the wall and onto the baseboard.

"Coffee," Charlie said lamely.

The old man pursed his lips. "Now I have to paint."

"Go ahead," Charlie said. "Paint the whole fucking apartment."

Mr. Grunner slowly raised his gaze to Charlie's sweaty face. His eyes blazed. "Filthy mouth," he said.

After a long silence, Frank said, "You're quite the diplomat, Charlie."

Mr. Grunner's stare was scalding, and Charlie looked away. "Sorry. I lost my temper."

Mr. Grunner gestured dismissively with his hand and said, "I think you lost everything."

Later, while Charlie was making a list of things he had to do before he left, Frank said, "Two hundred dollars is a hell of a lot for painting this apartment, Charlie."

Charlie went on with his list as if he hadn't heard. When he finally answered, his voice was frayed. "He would've haggled all day, and I'm exhausted." He put his pen down. "That stain isn't from coffee, you know. When I was on the booze, I puked on the wall and just left it there for a week."

Frank suggested that Charlie stay the night with him and his wife, but Charlie said he wanted to leave Calgary the way he came – in a cab. "I want to feel my business is finished, as if I was at a convention or something."

"I understand," Frank said, though Charlie could see that he didn't.

Charlie had difficulty feeling grateful to Frank, who hadn't finished high school and now worked graveyard shift as a janitor at K Mart. At AA meetings, Frank often joked about his lack of education: "I tried to study, but it was too noisy in the bar."

Whenever his deliberate, flat voice announced, "My name's Frank and I'm an alcoholic," Charlie groaned to himself. Frank's AA talks were a mix of the usual slogans – *Let Go and Let God*, *Easy Does It* – and smarmy anecdotes. Charlie hated to think what Frank would have been like with a few drinks under his belt.

His wife Lina was obese, yet she wore tight polyester slacks and T-shirts with slogans like *I'm Ready If You Are* or *World's Greatest Lover*. Her laugh was like sandpaper, and she called every man she knew – except Frank – "Honey." "You're looking long in the tooth, Honey," she'd say to Charlie after a meeting, slapping him on the back.

Charlie sometimes imagined waking in the night next to Lina's sleep-laden bulk: it would be like drowning, like sinking in mud. But to Frank, Lina was a kind of homespun goddess. "She has the joy of living," he told Charlie once. "After all she's been through, she can still thank God every morning for letting her see another day."

Charlie didn't want to know what Lina had been through.

An hour after Frank had left, Charlie was staring at the telephone, sweat trickling from his armpits. He had begun dialling Nancy's number several times, but quit when he doubted he could control his voice.

For a long time he held the telephone in his lap and talked himself out of ordering a quart of Johnny Walker from a taxi company. He forced up sweaty recollections of his first few days in the treatment centre, days of seared nerves and thudding panic. When he had finally crawled out of a lurid bout of the DTs, it was as if he hadn't heard a human voice for months. He had been parched, and the nurses had all spoken to him with warm, liquid voices.

Finally he dialled Nancy's number. When someone picked up the phone, Charlie realized he hadn't considered what to do if one of the kids answered: both were old enough to at least take a message. He decided he would hang up.

"Hello. Nancy Hansford speaking."

Nancy's generically cheerful voice immediately put Charlie on edge. Throughout the long crisis that had been their marriage, she had almost never lost control, while Charlie had always been either shouting or reaching for a drink.

"Hello?" Nancy repeated.

Charlie felt sweat soaking through his shirt. His cigarette was so damp it was falling apart; he tossed the remnants in the ashtray. "This is Charlie, Nancy."

There was a long pause. "You're sober?"

"I just got out of a treatment centre."

"Who put you in?"

"I did."

Nancy sighed. "All right. Keep talking."

"I'm coming back to Toronto."

"When?"

"Tomorrow morning. I have a flight booked."

The line was silent for a moment. Finally Nancy said, "What do you want from me, Charlie?"

Charlie was holding the phone so tightly his hand had begun to cramp. "I just want to see you and the kids. That's all."

"I have to think about this."

"Of course."

"Where are you staying?"

"At Jeff's, I guess." Charlie hadn't talked to his younger brother for months, but Jeff was always good for a place on the couch, if nothing else.

"I'll call there tomorrow night, Charlie."

Charlie didn't want to let her get away so quickly. "Nancy?" he said. "How are the kids, Nancy?"

But she had hung up.

Later, Charlie was too wired to sleep, so he carried a kitchen chair to the living-room window and stared blearily into the neighbour's back yard, half lit by the spotlights of Charlie's building. A heavy rain swept against the window, through the glaring arc of the spotlights.

In the neighbour's yard, a rusted-out Oldsmobile was up on concrete blocks; mismatched tires were heaped by the sagging wooden fence. Charlie was reminded unwillingly of the house he had grown up in. A hand-wring washing machine had leaned against the back porch of this house for years, half hidden by tall thistly weeds and scraps of weathered lumber.

Laying his forehead on the window sill, Charlie fell asleep. When he awoke, his head was throbbing and his back was coated with a cold, oily sweat. It was two in the morning. The rain had stopped.

Charlie dragged himself into the bathroom and stiffly undressed. Before stepping into the shower, he glanced uneasily at his reflection in the grimy full-length mirror on the door. His ribs seemed about to slice through his lustreless skin; his legs and arms were like bundles of twigs; and his flushed, gaunt face was alive with tics and tremors. Charlie was thirty-three, but at the treatment centre the duty nurse had scribbled on his admittance chart, *Age 45*?

He ran the water hot as he could stand it, then leaned against the ceramic tile wall, closing his eyes. For a few moments he was able to enjoy the deep coolness of the tiles against his shoulder and arms, the scouring of the water on his chest. This freedom from turmoil was so rare its sudden presence moved him almost to tears. Would he ever feel it for more than a few minutes at a time?

The cab driver, a large, rumpled man with a sagging face, offered to carry Charlie's two boxes and suitcase to the cab. "I'm George," he said, gripping Charlie's hand.

In the cab, George asked where Charlie was headed, then said, "Toronto's too big for me. You get stabbed and the neighbours just step over you, like in New York. I read last week about a woman in New York that got raped three times in one day." Half listening, Charlie watched George talk: the driver shifted his weight constantly, drew hungrily on a cigarette, swivelled his eyes, licked his lips. Yet he was merely telling Charlie about a neighbour's plumbing business. "He's got the western suburbs sewn up," he was saying. "He bought an old guy's clients, like doctors do. And believe me, a good plumber makes one hell of a pile of money."

At the airport, after helping carry Charlie's baggage to the counter, George was gulping for breath; sweat ran down his flushed face. Charlie gave him a large tip and asked, "You okay?"

George took out a handkerchief and wiped his face. "Sure. My doctor says I'll live to be a hundred." He folded Charlie's money and tucked it into a pocket. "You got family in T.O.?"

"Sort of," Charlie said.

George nodded. "I know what you mean."

For half an hour Charlie chain-smoked in the almost empty departure lounge, staring through the long windows at the grey tarmac. He tried to make plans for Toronto, but these quickly became unruly fragments. His stomach was churning; sweat beaded on his forehead, prickling his scalp.

The handful of other passengers waiting for the Toronto flight all looked purposeful, legitimate, and Charlie suddenly regretted turning down Frank's offer of a drive to the airport. Why was he always manoeuvring himself into isolation? He had always loathed being offered help or advice, it enraged him. Last night, Frank had written his phone number on a scrap of paper which Charlie had immediately tossed into the garbage. Yet he remembered the number, he had called it so many times in his first week out of the centre.

The air in the narrow cabin of the jet was stale and overheated, and as Charlie edged toward his seat, he felt as if his lungs were shrinking. His head ached dully. He dreaded a four-hour flight, particularly without cigarettes.

He hadn't thought to ask for an aisle or window seat when he booked his flight, and when he saw that he was between an elderly couple and a young boy, he was furious. Fortunately there was no stewardess or steward in sight, and he had time to calm down. He didn't want to make an asshole of himself before the plane had left the ground.

To get into his seat, Charlie pressed past the old man and then the old woman, who was soundlessly asleep, slack mouth gaping. The old man looked once at Charlie, sniffed, then turned away; his grey face made Charlie think of a wet newspaper.

His anger abating, Charlie hunched into his seat, assailed by humiliating memories of his behaviour at the treatment centre. This had been a long, barracks-like building, sparsely furnished. The rooms were all grey or white. For most of his month there, Charlie had been in tatters emotionally, crying tenderly one moment, in a senseless rage the next. Every day had been like a bout of the dry heaves. Yet on the morning of his discharge, Charlie had felt miraculously chastened and cleansed. He had been swollen with hope.

What had happened to that clarity? Frank would say, You have to go to AA meetings, use the phone, pray. But Charlie was hanging on to sobriety by his fingertips, and what had helped the old AA hands was for him wincingly banal – the Twelve Steps like a Hallmark greeting card, the Higher Power no more plausible than the Father, the Son, and the Holy Ghost. Before booze had sunk Charlie, he had been a good freelance technical writer – always precise and sparing – and his training had, he felt, made him immune to empty phrases.

The thin, frail boy beside Charlie sighed and pulled his bare legs onto his seat. Charlie had been staring into space for some time, but now he glanced at the boy, who had begun to tap his small fingers nervously on the armrest.

The boy's skin was pale as wet bone; his hair was glossy black. He had a sweetish, faintly milky scent. His pale green eyes reminded Charlie uncomfortably of his own son, Graham.

On Charlie's long list of things he would prefer to not think about, Graham was at the top. As a father Charlie had been a calamity, a natural disaster – Graham's neediness had repelled and embarrassed him. His chief project in Toronto would be to present Graham with a sober and much improved father. So far, Charlie knew, he was only sober.

Nancy wasn't going to make his new life easy. Thinking of the long list of injustices she could – and no doubt would – cite against him, Charlie shook his head. He and Nancy had practised marital discord on the grand scale, yet when she had finally thrown him out, Charlie's sense of outrage had been so keen he could scarcely believe no one shared it. "You told me yourself that you fight every night," one of his drinking buddies had observed. "What did you expect?"

"She changed the fucking locks!" Charlie shouted. "When I came home, my key didn't fit."

The other man had shrugged. "Count your blessings. My wife tried to have me committed."

Charlie glanced at his watch; the flight was at least twenty minutes behind schedule. As if anticipating takeoff, his ears had begun to plug. The boy was still tapping his fingers on the armrest.

At the front of the cabin, a stewardess began a bored demonstration of the life jackets and safety equipment. She was lanky, pretty, and Charlie's lust flared. Alcohol had for years doused his other appetites, but in the last few weeks Charlie had masturbated so often a blister-like sore had formed on his penis. To hide his erection, Charlie took a magazine from the seat rack and laid it in his lap. A moment later the old woman, still asleep, began to gurgle like a clogged drain. Charlie scowled.

The boy noticed this and whispered, "She told *me* to be quiet."

Charlie smiled weakly. He didn't feel like chatting, particularly with a kid, but the only alternative was four uninterrupted hours with his own dismal thoughts.

The jet began to thud and rattle down the runway. The boy had fastened his seatbelt, but he fumbled anxiously with a pile of comic books. Charlie said, "Let me help."

He tucked the comics under the boy's seat an instant before the jet lurched into the air. During the first few minutes of ascent, the boy closed his eyes and gripped the armrest so tightly his small knuckles went white. Charlie remembered that Graham sometimes slept with his teeth clenched.

"First time you've flown?" Charlie asked when the boy had opened his eyes.

The boy nodded.

"Takeoff is the worst part. And landing," Charlie said. "The rest is easy."

A few minutes later, the jet began to level out; pale blue sky and banners of cloud streamed past the boy's small window. His mouth open, the boy stared down at the city and its surrounding hills.

"We're five thousand feet up," Charlie said quietly. "A mile."

"Wow. How high will we get?"

"About five miles."

The boy shivered with pleasure. He took his eyes away from the window to glance at Charlie. "How come you know about jets?"

"I read a lot."

Apparently this was a startling response for the boy: his eyes widened. "My father doesn't like to read."

"He's missing a lot."

The boy nodded non-committally.

On an impulse, Charlie offered his flushed, sweaty hand. "I'm Charlie."

"I'm Ryan," the boy replied solemnly. His hand was slight, cool.

"How do you do, Ryan?" Charlie said.

Ryan smiled shyly.

Charlie suddenly thought: Why is he alone? Aren't kids supposed to have adults with them?

"I'm going to visit my dad," the boy said. "He got married again. Have you ever been to Toronto?"

"I used to live there."

"Did you like it?"

"No," Charlie conceded. He paused. "But there's lots to do."

Ryan nodded happily, then looked puzzled. "How come you didn't like it?"

"I'm not sure."

Charlie was unwilling to think of Toronto in detail. He

could afford only a dump of an apartment, maybe a furnished room, and looking for work would demand reserves of humility he did not at the moment possess. Somehow he would have to stay sober.

Ryan reached under his seat for a comic book. Charlie glanced at the cover, which showed an American helicopter exploding at the edge of a jungle clearing as Asian soldiers lurked nearby: *Tales From Nam.* Lacking the energy for moral outrage, Charlie sighed and closed his eyes.

Soon he had drifted into a brittle sleep crowded with rattling thuds, with draughts of clammy air on his face and hands. He awoke with a start to a clatter of bottles and cans – at the front of the aisle, a stewardess was wheeling out the drink cart.

Charlie grasped instantly that by refusing to let his week-long anticipation of this moment become conscious, he had hoped to be able to say, It just happened. I was caught off guard. From the moment he had called the airline, he had planned to get drunk. His mouth was painfully dry, his hands trembled. Closing his eyes, he saw Frank's weary, tolerant face, his mild, unsurprised eyes. *Drunks are all alike, Charlie.*

The cart's rattling seemed to be occurring inside Charlie's skull. When the stewardess had reached Charlie's row of seats, he opened his eyes suddenly, gasping.

Ryan was staring. "What's wrong?"

"Nothing," Charlie said. Ryan frowned, and Charlie quickly corrected himself. "I'm a bit sick. From the flight."

"Like being seasick?"

Charlie nodded.

The old woman was awake, and she testily demanded ice-water for herself and her husband. When the stewardess handed her a plastic cup, she said, "These ice cubes are too small." Ryan looked at Charlie and rolled his eyes.

"And what will you gentlemen have?" the stewardess asked.

"A Coke," Ryan said.

"One Coke," the stewardess said brightly.

After a long pause, Charlie licked his lips and said, "I'll have the same."

When Ryan went back to his grisly comic, Charlie again slid into sleep. He woke to Ryan whispering, "Are you awake, Charlie?"

"Uh huh."

The boy turned to the window. "Look. You can see forever. Where are we?"

Charlie craned his neck to see a long stretch of square fields bordered by dirt roads. Farmhouses and barns were tiny dots. On the edge of the horizon, the brilliant blue of the sky softened to a white haze. It seemed to Charlie that he could actually see the curve of the earth.

"We're above the prairies," he said. "Manitoba, maybe."

"It's so *huge.*"

Despite Ryan's excitement, he soon drifted into uneasy sleep himself. He shifted position so often Charlie was surprised he didn't wake himself. Occasionally his head jerked sharply, as if from a slap.

Charlie went to the tiny bathroom to wipe sweat from his face. On the way back he nearly fainted: he caught the edge of a seat and leaned against it until his legs would support him. A young woman in a grey business outfit glared at him, and after a moment Charlie understood that she thought he was drunk.

Back in his seat, Charlie again wiped sweat from his face. He was parched, his head was throbbing.

What am I doing? he asked himself harshly. He should have listened to Frank. As soon as I get off the plane, Charlie vowed, I'll call him.

Ryan had awakened and was again staring at Charlie. "You're sweating," he said, his small face pinched with worry. "What's wrong?"

Charlie touched the sweat on his forehead, then looked at his fingers as if they were bloody. "I'm afraid," he said impulsively.

Ryan nodded. "So am I."

"Everyone's afraid," Charlie said.

Then he laughed, and so did Ryan.

ALISON WEARING

Notes from Under Water

November 11, 1990

Today someone asked me how I got this job. He was American. I could tell by the way he said college. As though it were spelled with an *a* not an *o*. How does anyone get a job in a free, democratically-elected government? I asked him. Nepotism. Jesus, how do you think I got this job?

November 16

Advisor, they call me. I can barely keep a straight face just saying it. But I'm not doing a bad job of acting it. Advisor on environmental and foreign affairs. This is theatre of the absurd.

November 19

It is the anniversary of the revolution, the one with the texture of thick curtains. The kind that hide a stage. The revolution of peaceful negotiations and a happy ending. The stuff of films; maybe a play. The revolution of students, of musicians, of writers from the underground. The Velvet Underground.

One year ago, Wenceslas Square echoed with the chanting of tens of thousands of people. DUBCEK DUBCEK! HAVEL HAVEL!! They had the determination that comes with desperation, the tenacity that speaks the words *I will die for this*. I can't imagine the power of a nation of people ready to say this. But isn't this why I came here? Because I want to be able to imagine this. And I wanted to live in a country where artists were running the show.

Today's anniversary celebrations were a let-down. Wenceslas Square was so jammed with people that at one point I was suspended, my feet dangling just a bit above the ground. The star attraction was George Bush or *George Bushi,* as his name appeared on the publicity posters. His nasal voice welcomed Czechs and Slovaks into the world of capitalism and democracy. The New World Order. Rent to Own. *Yankee Doodle Dandy* blared from the speakers mounted on light posts. Freedom is just around the corner, Bushi told us. But which corner, I wonder. Which, uh, which corner?

November 26

I have started meeting the foreign affairs boys for breakfast on Tuesdays and Thursdays. Miroslav, Jaroslav and Rostislav. The Slavs. Miroslav always has the same thing. They all do. Blood sausage and beer. I have coffee. Now that you are part of the Western world, I told them today – they smiled – you should have English names. They liked this idea. Miroslav, I said. Your name will be Larry. Jaroslav, let me see . . . do you like the name Moe? All right, and Rostislav, you can be Curly. Curly? he said. I like this name.

I meet the other boys whenever they have a spare moment, which is normally in the evening and normally in a pub. I like this job. Emil doesn't want to talk about work after work. He wants to learn English. He can barely say boo. Maggie Thatcher is a monster with tits, he repeated tonight over our third litre of beer. Memorize that, I told him, and I will teach you something else the next time.

Sasa is much more serious about his job. I enjoy these meetings less. We talk about ecology and atomic energy, and I feel myself ranting like an ecoterrorist. I told him he should start a counter-revolutionary group: the Khmer Vert. Recycle or die. But he said he is tired of revolutions. He's very, uh, *concerned.* And I'm, uh not. Not anymore. Not after he took me to that national park in the north. Where we drove for twenty minutes and didn't see a single tree with leaves. Just black trunks and branches. Skeletons, I kept saying in the car. The black orchard, he called it in his speech to parliament the following week. I watched him standing there giving his speech and talking as if he were holding the bones in his hand. It was eerie. I decided never to be so concerned. I don't want to end up holding a skeleton.

The thing about Sasa is that I have this feeling we'll end up together. In bed, I mean. This is my prediction. It's not really something concerned married men normally do, but people do strange things when they've got bones in their hands. I just have this feeling.

Then there is Zdenek. Zdenek is halfway between Emil and Sasa. We also have meetings in pubs, but he's only semi-concerned. Like me. He told me he thinks Thatcher would be the ideal leader of this country, if only she spoke Czech. Most people agree with me, he said, and I believe him. I heard the statue debate, but had to leave because I was frothing at the mouth. What it is, frothy at mouth? he asked. I said it was another way of saying angry. Frothy, he muttered and scribbled in his notebook. I'm not sure about that either, he said. It is true that Reagan is liberator of Eastern Europe, but erecting statue of him should not be priority in our parliament. Not this year. I ordered another beer and peeled skin from the inside of my cheek with my teeth.

Emil, Sasa, and Zdenek. The Slav Nots.

November 29

I live on the same street as the U.S. Ambassador. She is the personification of U.S. politics. Her name is Shirley Temple Black.

One of her embassy workers was introduced to me today in parliament. A fellow capitalist, he said. Everyone laughed. I picked wax out of my ear. Once everyone had gone into session, he told me a joke. How many Czechs does it take to screw in a light bulb? (Shrug.) None. The Germans will do it for them. (Smile.) He leaned a bit closer. If we don't get there first. Then he winked and walked away.

I went outside to the top of Wenceslas Square. The sun was shining and the roof of the National Museum looked like liquid gold. I stood there for a moment. Smiling. God, I love this city, I thought. If Paris could see this, she would be ashamed to show her face. I saw a crowd outside a shop and skipped down to join the line. It wasn't until I was right up next to the window that I recognized them. Freedom muffins, they were called. Huge bran muffins stuck with toothpicks that waved mini-American flags.

December 1

This language has far too many consonants for its own good. I learned the word for ice cream today: zmrzlina. And I thought, why bother even having the i and a? Why not just go the whole nine yards and eliminate *all* vowels? With words like v and s, we seem to be well on our way already. And how do you say Thursday again? Oh yeah, Ctvrtek.

Czech has a letter that exists in no other language: the ř. You say it by making a nice rolling *r* at the front of the mouth. The way people from Puerto Rico say Puerto Rrrico. Rrrrrr. That's it. Now, *while keeping that r spinning behind your teeth*, say the letter j. Yeah, the letter j. At the same time. Rjrjrjrjrj. Go and practise that and I'll teach you something else the next time.

I saw Emil as I was leaving the dining room this morning. He smiled from across the hallway and ran his fingers across his forehead. Then he walked over to me and pointed his finger right at my nose. Tat-cher ees mon-ster wid *teats*. Excellent, I said. Your pronunciation is even better than mine.

December 4

The only thing that I don't like about this county is that, well, everybody's white. And I don't just mean white. I mean painful-not-even-a-hint-of-oh-I-dunno-maybe-light-pink-white. And I mean everybody. When I ride the economy-size escalator down into the subway, I look over at the people riding up: white, white, white, glowing, translucent, painful to look at, white, white, white. They all look like statues. Carved out of cream cheese. Yeah, that's it exactly, because the texture of their skin is that same mushy, pliable drop-it-on-the-floor-and-it-will-just-go-blaaab consistency. The capital of this country should be Philadelphia. I wonder what people in Philadelphia look like.

December 17

I can't get this cheese thing out of my mind. The other day I saw a guy – not in the subway, in a tram – who looked like he had been carved out of, I'm not kidding, blue cheese. It was almost like all his blood just stopped flowing while he stood there. Blue. Like a vein. So there I was thinking this and we stopped outside the national theatre. A lot more people got on. There was all this shoving and pushing and he was edged right over to where I was sitting. Our knees were touching. When I looked up, I looked at his armpit. And get this. He even *smelled* like blue cheese. For the rest of the ride I sat there in sort of a gorgonzola daze. Just outside the castle, I squeezed out of the tram like I was coming out of one of those plastic rolls of processed cheese they used to sell (maybe they still do.) And guess what I did next. I looked down at my knee to see if there was any mould on it.

December 20

This is getting out of hand. I'm already having difficulty looking at people without words like gouda and mozzarella coming into my mind, but today it got worse. There we were at breakfast, talking about something. The Charter of Rights and Freedoms? I was improvising. I looked over at Rostislav (Curly) and my eyes fixed on his stomach. His huge, round, barley belly. Before I knew it I was remembering my friend Theo. The time he told me about slicing into a cadaver's intestines and bowels. (He was a medical student.) He told me – and he explained that this happens when you don't eat enough fibre – that this guy's bowels were all full of *dried faecal matter*. I'll never forget it. That some of this stuff had been stuck there for *years*. And there's Curly, eating blood sausage and beer at seven in the morning. And I'm wondering how much of that large gut is made up of dried faecal matter. Yeah, it was the Charter of Rights and Freedoms. I remember now.

December 24

Memories of age eight: sunrise mornings in a thin wool sweater with buttons like hard candy, and a cat. I wonder what I was thinking about with my bony knees tucked under my chin? Unstructured thoughts of solitude.

Merry Christmas.

December 31

Tomorrow most of the subsidies will be removed from staple items. We are entering a free market economy. Please put your seats in the upright position, lock your tray in front of you and be sure that your seatbelts are securely fastened. Extinguish all cigarettes. This is a non-smoking flight.

January 1, 1991

A ride on the metro is four times more expensive than yesterday. Bread and milk are also up. Toilet paper is being sold for 8kcs per roll, or 4 for 35 kcs. I now earn the equivalent of 70 bottles of wine per month.

January 10

The American. The one who asked me how I got this job. He was all dressed up in a suit and dying to tell me why, I could tell. So I didn't ask. He told me anyway. Guess what? he said. I got a job. Yeah, I'm teaching business, and English, of course. That's nice – trying to sound even more bored than I felt – where? Oh, it's a new place. Just opened. It's called The Freedom Learning Centre.

I think I went into shock. The Freedom Learning Centre. I could think of nothing to say. I just frothed at the mouth and wiped it away with my sleeve. My name is Vaughan, he said with an outstretched hand and a smile that was all lips, no teeth. He said he really admired what I was doing here, and I almost asked him what that was. Before I knew it, he had asked me if I wanted to go to a party. The next part was almost an out-of-body experience. As if all of my intelligence and rational thought left me for a moment. I said *sure*.

January 11

drowning in a room of recycled conversations with uninteresting people who say things like "good for you!" and are overexcitable or groups of Eurail groupies who make me feel forty the way they giggle and recount their meagre adventures like anyone really gives a shit.

January 15, 1991

I ran into that American embassy worker in parliament this morning. I wished him a happy Martin Luther King Day and said I had a joke for him. How may Americans does it take to screw in a light bulb? He smiled and said, I dunno. One. But it takes the whole fucking military to keep the furnace on.

I don't think he got it. But I'll bet he gets his news from CNN. Imagine. Watching CNN and thinking you were getting the news.

January 16

i wonder what a fish feels like
when one of its bowlmates dies
and floats to the top
it must be what war feels like

January 25

The boys were in a good mood this morning. Larry and Curly are going on a diplomatic mission to South East Asia. They will try to sell some of this country's heavy industry – we must keep the Europe clean, they told me – and to sell weapons. This is Slovakia's main industry, someone explained, and without it they would have nothing. Weapons are weapons. If we don't sell them, someone else will. If we stopped, the Slovaks would raise hell. They are backward people. Just like the Gypsies. They even collaborated with fascists. The Czechs were the most advanced people in Europe. Also one of the richest. At this point I stopped listening.

Two identity crises make a nation. A nation about to get swallowed.

February 5

I skip around parliament. Run up and down the hollow staircases. Play in the elevator of the adult world. Where I never belonged. And with any luck never will. I am the child who would beg to go to the university on weekends. To play in the empty hallways while my Dad worked in his office. The smell of musty concrete, the feel of crusty carpets. Hallways that echoed. Empty rooms full of voices. I spun out of every adventure with rug burns on my elbows. From diving into imaginary pools.

February 11

Sasa took me to his old school. Where he taught before he became a politician. He said he would like me to talk to the students about Canada. Talk about Canada, I thought. That should be easy. But when I stood there in front of a room full of seven-year-olds, all I could think about were pancakes and the GST. I decided to teach them a song. *Oh I'm a lumberjack and I'm OK, I sleep all night and I work all day. I cut down trees, I eat my lunch, I go to the lavat'ry. On Wednesdays I go shopping, and have buttered scones for tea.* I almost wet my pants. Everybody was laughing and no one knew why. God I love this country. Then I asked them to make a painting about Czechoslovakia. Something from their own imagination. I told them I would send their paintings to a school in Canada. Sasa and I skipped down the street for beer and dumplings. He told me I was crazy. That I should never have children. I agreed on both accounts. When we came back to pick up the paintings, I felt like someone had driven a knife into my stomach. Every single child had painted a factory.

We went out afterwards to a pub. To cheer ourselves up with some of the world's finest tasting depressant. Sasa talked to the barman and ordered something called Pradjed. You will like this, he said. It is alcohol with a human face.

February 14

I ran into Vaughan again. Actually he ran into me. I was sitting in that pretentious café. Sitting there looking out the window at the river when he came over with a whole group of people – I think there were three of them – and just sat down. You look like you could use some company, he said. I swallowed froth. We all teach at The Centre, said one of the group-people. Has anyone learned freedom yet? I asked. Silence. They all just sat there looking exquisitely bored.

Then the conversation started. The *conversation.* They spoke about nothing in particular. In particular, they spoke about nothing. Post-modern feminism in a post-post-modern-feminist society. From a post-Marxist perspective. It was riveting. What do *you* think? one of them asked me. I wanted to make a pseudo-intellectual comment, something with the word "deconstruct" in it, just to show them I could play their stupid game. But something happened. I couldn't do it. Couldn't get the words out. I just sat there, looking into the centre of the table, listening to them blow smoke rings around my head.

I decided to escape to the washroom during the next lull in the conversation. It was almost immediate. I went downstairs, put 50 *heller* in the dish on the table, and the old woman at the door handed me three sheets of toilet paper. One at a time. As she flicked her finger around in the dish of coins, I wondered what would happen to these prices in a free market economy. It could become twice as expensive to pee, (assuming bodily functions had been subsidized), or we might just get fewer sheets of toilet paper to do the same job. Perhaps The Freedom Learning Centre was teaching this sort of thing in its classes.

When I came back to the table, they had changed the subject. Now they were talking about books. All the right books. And I wasn't sure I read any of those. Every one of them was in black I wanted to ask what they were mourning. Surely not the death of communism. Maybe they were mourning freedom. They wore scarves and politically-correct jewellery. Sat in sophisticated positions and smoked Marlboros. The women wore blood-red lipstick and made their mouths look like baboon asses. I'm doing this teaching now, one of them started, but actually I'm a writer. Everyone in this goddamn town is a writer, I screamed to myself. No. Everybody is *actually*-I'm-a-writer. I'm taking a year off to travel, but *actually* I'm a writer. I work for an advertising firm at the moment, but *actually* . . . I will never say that, I decided. Actually, I'm a bus driver. I'm just hanging around this café until I can get a route.

One of them asked me if I missed Toronto. She said Toronto as though it had three syllables. Everybody knows it only has two: Traw-no. And I said, miss Toronto? That's like asking someone if they miss having planters warts. Everybody looked really puzzled. Like they all felt sorry for me. Like I had just said something so strange that *they* were embarrassed. How could I miss a place where café culture is coffee in a styrofoam cup with a travel lid to drink on the subway? Dumb American.

Disjointed conversations with people I care nothing for make me taste loneliness like a mouthful of chalkdust. The work conversation was too generous. It was more like breathing with sound effects.

February 21

"When one joins in song with others it is like being drawn on by a fish hook." I wonder if Kafka ever introduced himself as an actually-I'm-a-writer.

March 5

The boys are back from Asia. Malaysia was incredible, they said. Just like a paradise. How will it look after they have all of your heavy industry? I wanted to ask, but didn't. Where else did you go? I asked instead. They looked down at their breakfast, gave each other a sideways glance and started to laugh. Bangkok. They could barely contain themselves. You wouldn't believe it. What those girls can do with their, you know . . . I pretended I didn't know. Shooting ping pong balls across the room, and drinking Coca-Cola, but not with their mouths. I felt that same frothing coming on again, so I told them I had to leave early today.

Bangkok. Banged cock.

I saw Sasa on Wenceslas Square. He asked me if everything was OK. I wanted to say, sure. No problem. But when I went to speak, I could feel my eyes fill up with water. I must have looked pathetic. Pathetic. Because the next thing I remember is the weight of his hand on the back of my head, and the smell of his jacket. It smelled like coal. And then being here. God, I thought this might happen, but I – uh – didn't think this would happen.

March 26

I spent the whole day on the island, sitting on a tree stump, hanging out with the swans. I've heard they're monogamous. Hard to believe. Even harder to believe that someone sat down and figured it out. Biologists are almost as boring as academics. Spending their whole lives studying life without ever living. I wonder how swans feel about adultery.

April 10

I could see myself ranting, but could barely hear a word. I was character acting. I could see it. He couldn't. He thought it was real. But I knew I was just acting out a scene from a bad play. Or a good play. I couldn't tell. I'm so used to acting that I don't even know when I'm doing it anymore. Pretending that this doesn't mean anything. That he hasn't crawled inside of me. That I haven't felt him breathing, inside of me.

April 15

He called in the afternoon and said he was having a bad day. He had lost all of his identification. Couldn't even get into parliament. A few minutes later he was here again. I could have done without this, but afternoon sex with him was something I decided I wanted to investigate. Bad idea. It was awkward. Boring. I was about as far from an orgasm as I was from Toronto. About seven hours. By jet. Suddenly, everything went sour. I feel so guilty, he said. It is easy for you. You do not have somebody. But me, I feel terrible. I said something from a bad movie. He said he would call later. He didn't.

It is easy for me. Actually.

April 25

He said he thought I was clever. That I wouldn't let this happen. He was wrong. I used to be clever. Back in the days when I thought things worked. Now I know they don't.

April 27

I got a telegram today. Second one of my life. The first one was way back when I was a Eurail groupie. When I giggled and recounted my meagre adventures like anyone really gave a shit. That was my first telegram and I don't even remember what it said. But I remember I got it in Switzerland because the man who gave it to me called me fräulein. Or maybe I was in Germany. Anyway I remember thinking, *I don't feel like a fräulein.* God, does anyone?

The telegram I got today was one I will never forget. It said, FEEL LIKE A PICNIC? CALL ME COLLECT. And then a long number. No name. No clues. I live for shit like this.

I went to the phone and tried to call this long number collect. But an international operator came on the line. I'm sorry, she said. You can't call this number collect. This is a number in China. Jesus, I said to her. This gets better all the time. I don't even *know* anyone in China. I smeared my thumb against the little knobs where you replace the receiver and I started dialling the moment I got a dial tone. I never stopped and thought: should I spend one fifth of my salary calling someone I don't know in China? I just did it. Hullo? It was a male voice. It sounded American. Hi, I said. I just received a telegram telling me to come there. Do you know anything about this? Oh yeah, he said. Hold on a sec. Definitely American.

It seemed so strange to talk to him again. So strange, because it wasn't so strange at all. You would think that after all this time, it would be strange. But it wasn't. He sounds the same. He is the same. Everybody is always the same, no matter how different they sound, or how different they say they are. Something to remember.

I am tired of this place. Tired of this. I am tired of breathing air that tastes like coal, washing my hair and having the suds turn black, waking up in the morning and spitting black phlegm into the sink. I am tired of this job. Tired of spewing out words of democratic wisdom, of giving advice I am unqualified to give, of making fun of people who are only looking for something better than they had. I am tired of being someone's affair. Tired of being emotionally controlled by someone over whom I have no control. Sometimes I wonder if I will ever be anything but someone else's adventure.

At the moment, I can't think of a single reason why I shouldn't go to China for a picnic. No reason at all.

I haven't felt this good since I skipped Toronto to come here.

May 8

It's settled. Flying was out from the very beginning. Flying is boring. You go to the airport, board the plane, fly, land. Bolshoi dealski. So I went to the train station and I lined up with everybody else. I heard people ahead of me buying tickets to Warsaw, Budapest, Berlin. I got to the front and said I'd like a ticket to Beijing. The woman behind the glass thought I was some sort of prankster. Funny fucking foreigner. No really, I said and tried to look serious. I had a bit of difficulty with this because even I couldn't believe I was serious. She shook her head and mumbled something to the woman working beside her. This woman pressed her face to the glass and looked me up and down. Send her down, I heard her say. For a split second I thought this was a slang term for *arrest her*, but I put this out of my mind. This country has a free, democratically-elected government, I reassured myself. Just like Reagan's America, Thatcher's Britain, Hitler's Germany. What am I worrying about?

I went down, as it were, to an office that didn't seem to have much of a function outside of the fact that I was there wanting a train ticket to China. There were three people who worked, as it were, there. They were all sitting around drinking coffee and giving me the same look as the woman upstairs. Not the one with her face smushed against the glass, the other one. I sat down and made it look like I was not going to move until they gave me this goddamn ticket. Finally someone put down their coffee. Ninety minutes later I left with a ticket to China in my hand. I love it when I decide to do something without making a decision. On my way home I imagined what it would be like to have a permanent address. It must feel like stapling your hand to a wall.

May 14

I went back to the same office. The same people were drinking the same coffee and giving me the same look. Look, they said to each other. She's back. I tried to look serious. For some reason, it was even more difficult now that I had the ticket in my hand. I need to know when the train is going to arrive, I told them. Someone is meeting me in Beijing. The Prague to Moscow portion was no problem. It was the Moscow to Beijing *via Siberia* part that seemed to cause a bit of trouble.

I went home and called the long number again. The same American voice. Yeah, hold on a sec. Look, I said, you can't meet me at the station. My train has no time of arrival. Maybe six days, they told me at the office. Maybe eight days. If civil war in Soviet Union, maybe a few more days. Neither of us knew a good meeting place in Beijing, although for a moment I actually paused like maybe one would come to me. Yeah, that sounds good. Under the portrait of Chairman Mao in Tienanmen Square every night at six o'clock, starting from eight days after I leave Prague. OK, I said, see you there.

May 23

Today I went to the train station and sat down on the stone seats. The ones where all the homeless people, who aren't homeless people because this county doesn't have any, sleep. I sat with them and I stared up at the departure board watching the letters and numbers shuffle as trains came and left. And I sat there wondering what all these not-really-homeless-people must think of all this coming and going. They, who have no homes to go to, watching us, who keep leaving ours. Funny. And I saw my train come up on the board. Moskva, it said. Seventeen thirteen. Track eight. I stared at it for a long time, because in one week I will be here with my bag, looking for track eight. A week or so after that I will be getting off in

Beijing. Funny. Berlin. Seventeen twenty-one. Track Six. Moskva. Seventeen Thirteen. Track eight.

May 25

He said it. The only thing worse than I love you. I *need* you. The word gives me a rash. A really sore one. Shingles. *Herpes zoster.* An acute viral disease affecting the ganglia of certain nerves. Characterized by inflammation, pain, and skin eruptions along the course of the affected nerve. He asked me if I needed him too. I said I would rather stop breathing. I did. But only for a few seconds. I told him I had quit my job and was leaving Prague. He laughed and said he didn't believe me. Kafka said that Prague doesn't let go, he told me. That only made me want to leave sooner. I told him I was going to Berlin. That I needed to be somewhere where I spoke the language. But I don't know why I said this because I don't speak German. Except fräulein. And I still don't feel like one.

I looked him straight in the eye and told him I was leaving in five days. Suddenly he believed me. His face looked like a grilled cheese sandwich. How dare you, he said through clenched teeth. I'm sure your wife would say the same to you, I replied.

May 29

echoing footsteps on cobblestone. speeding my pace. running. fists. clenched. pounding. a hand biting my arm. falling – both of us. forcing myself up. his head on the road. breathing fire. limping to a metro station. last train long gone. out-of-breath. hollow. phone-call-someone-anyone. ringing ringing ringing and seeing him. coming around the corner. *prague doesn't let go.* empty metro station. unlit park. dark bridge. construction site. nowhere.

a cab peeling off the bridge. screeching around me. full. not screaming. not able. a second cab. stopping. watching him across the street. diving in and locking the door. his fist against the window. home. collapsing onto the floor, into myself. knees tucked under my chin. rocking. rubbing my hands along my face. raw. like a rug burn. hands over arms. nails into skin. staring at the window to the street. the one that doesn't lock. not moving. not able. watching the sky and waiting for light. it will be thursday. *ctvrtek.* and i have a train to catch.

May 30

From my seat I see him. Standing on the next platform. Track Six. Berlin. Seventeen twenty-one. I feel nothing. Less than nothing. Like I'm floating to the top. As the train moves out of the station I watch the city rise into view. I face backwards. Watching my own departure. I put my feet on the seat in front of me. My hands cross over my stomach and hold one elbow in each palm. We pick up speed and the city spires sink, waving to me before they disappear. I am eased into the soothing rhythm of motion. Of being rocked to sleep. Of solitude. It is only when I close my eyes that I realize my hands are full of bones.

DOROTHY SPEAK

Relatives in Florida

At dinner, my brother Floyd says grace. "And, Dear Lord," he finishes up, "let us pray for our beloved father, who is in exile in the United States, and hope that he'll return to us someday."

"You don't know *where* he is," I say. "For all you know he's dead."

Father ran away ten years ago. I was twenty at the time, Floyd twenty-five. It wasn't until a few weeks after he disappeared that we realized he'd taken Floyd's credit card with him. We were able to trace his progress through the States by reading the credit card bill: a gasoline purchase in Watertown, New York. Dinner in Syracuse. Motel rooms in Pennsylvania, Maryland, Virginia.

"He's following the Interstate 81," I said, looking at a map. "He's taking his time. Probably headed for Florida."

"I hope he's not ill," Mother fretted, referring to a pharmacy purchase that showed up on the bill. She is a simple, unquestioning woman who does not always grasp the magnitude of things.

"Now," said Blanche happily, "we'll be able to tell people we have relatives in Florida."

Floyd, a small, flatulent man, a physical weakling with round wire-rimmed glasses and a red goatee, said he wasn't angry with Father for running up his credit card bill. "He didn't mean any harm," he said.

"You are a simpleton," I told him.

"If you were in touch with God," he said with gentle pity, "you'd know how to forgive."

Floyd got religion in his early twenties. He was working at the dairy then. He became so crazed with God that he went around the dairy exclaiming, "Praise the Lord, Brother! Halleluiah, Sister!" He sang hymns on the job. He tried to get a prayer group going at lunch break. One day he put religious pamphlets in the empty milk bottles riding down the conveyor belt. That was when they fired him.

Now he has worked his way up to lay preacher in the Church of the Risen Christ. He assists the minister, opens the church up on Sundays, counts the collection money, that sort of thing. He teaches Sunday school and gives the scripture readings at services. Once in awhile they let him give a sermon. For this, they pay him a small salary.

When I say that about Father being dead, they raise their eyes and look at me. It is an October evening and their faces are reflected in the black kitchen windows: Floyd with his stiff, Christian smile disclosing a mouthful of tiny, rotting teeth, Blanche batting her fleshy eyelids at me in disapproval, Mother swallowing a small, anxious, let's-not-fight gulp of air. At seventy, she has shrunken up to the size of a child, like a little figure in a picture book. On either side of her, Blanche and Floyd grip her bony hands, forming what Floyd calls a Chain of Prayer. Mother, her arms held high by them, wears an expression of surprise and reluctant salvation, like a suicide victim pulled from a river. She joined Floyd's church a year ago.

"You brought us up as atheists," I told her at the time. "How can you go against everything you ever taught us?"

"It's easier this way," she said. "Now Floyd leaves me alone. Maybe you should consider it."

"I'd sooner take poison."

Floyd and Blanche have a tiny apartment over near the bus depot but nearly every evening when I come home from work, I see Floyd's burgundy coupe parked in front of our place, a little frame house with a vestibule the size of a telephone booth stuck on the front. They say the apartment makes them restless, there's nothing to do there. I can't blame them for being bored with each other. Floyd reads the Bible all day and Blanche wants to look at television, but their set is broken. At our house, she sinks into an armchair, watches the game shows all afternoon, eats plates of Mother's lemon tarts. She is a big, soft woman with tufts of hair sprouting from the corners of her mouth like black grass.

"They need a child to distract them," Mother says.

"They're children themselves," I tell her.

"And Brethren," Floyd says at dinner, closing his eyes again, "let us bow our heads once more, for we are not finished with the Lord's work at this table. We will pray for our sister, Jean, that she may open her heart to the love of God –"

"I'm not going to sit here and listen to this rot," I declare, pushing my chair back. "You can pray until you're blue in the face and it won't change me."

"Pass the potatoes," says Blanche.

I pick up my plate and head for my room. It isn't the first time I've finished my dinner there. As I climb the stairs, I hear behind me Floyd's voice droning on in prayer, low and toneless, like the buzzing of a housefly. The sound of cutlery clattering on dinner plates rises to me through the floor. Later, I hear them cleaning up the dishes. Around nine o'clock, I hear the front door close. I go to the head of the stairs.

"Are the idiots gone?" I call down.

"Do you mean Floyd and Blanche?" Mother replies.

"Who else would I mean?"

Once, I thought they'd left and they hadn't. "Are the idiots gone?" I called down.

"No," Blanche answered without thinking, "we're still here."

On the weekends, Mother and I have a quiet life. Mother rises late and moves slowly from room to room in her mules and thick flannelette nightgown. She goes to the kitchen window and stands there for some time, motionless, looking out at the birdfeeder, at the chickadees, cardinals, bluejays, the hardy, faithful birds who will abide the Canadian winter with us. She is entertained by their bright wings, their swiftness, their greed. Her fingers, pressed to the cold windowsill as though frozen there, are white as bones. A circle of vapour forms on the glass where her face comes close to it. Later, she sits in her swivel rocker and says her prayers. Around noon she takes a bath in an inch of water. Fill the tub up, I tell her through the bathroom door. Spoil yourself. Enjoy your bath. I don't want to waste water, she says. Her skin has gotten very thin and silky and loose. Like an old suit that doesn't fit her anymore, it ripples and sags. There are big brown spots the size of pennies on the backs of her hands. She can pinch the skin there and pull it away a distance of an inch. The hair has fallen out of her arms and legs. She is smooth and much like a newborn baby, with this loose, wrinkled, hairless skin. In the afternoon, she puts on her clothes, thin sweaters that do not keep her warm. Thick ones are too heavy, she says. She cannot support them. They exhaust her. We turn up the thermostat on the living-room wall. She sits again in her chair and reads large-print books from the library, her legs extended straight out in front of her, supported by a footstool, her heels pressed together, the toes of her shoes pointing up at the ceiling. She reaches to turn on the radio.

On Saturday afternoon we wait for the rain to stop. Then we venture out onto the wet street, pulling our grocery buggy behind us. We turn onto a small sidewalk that cuts through our block to a larger street, where there is more traffic. We walk two blocks on cracked sidewalks, down a gradual slope to the store. There is a greyness to the day. Everything is grey: the low, woolly clouds, the shining road, the misty air.

The store, however, is bright and warm. We take a cart and pass up and down the aisles. The staff knows us. They say hello to Mother, hello to me. Clerks who were young men when I was a child now have grey hair, hearing aids, are big and round about the midriff. I cannot believe that they are still here, packing groceries into paper bags, stamping price stickers on cereal boxes, sweeping sawdust into little piles in the corners of the store. Perhaps they cannot believe that I am here shopping in the same grocery store I came to as a child.

The store hasn't changed in fifty years. First come the cereals and jams, then the tea and coffee, peanut butter, household cleaners and so on. Moving anything would upset the customers, elderly men and women who shuffle here from their nearby homes and apartments, leaning on canes, their glasses thick as bottles. This is a small store. There are newer ones now, big ones built further out, on the edge of town, chain stores large as factories, but they are for young people with families and cars, people who want fancy cheeses and delicatessen salads, who are not afraid of heavy grocery cart traffic, who do not distrust or become confused by technology.

At the meat counter, Mother picks up a pork roast and stares at it for a full minute, forgetting what it is she wants and where we are. Blood leaks through the cellophane wrapping onto her gloves. I move up behind her, take it from her hand and return it to the meat cooler.

She looks at me. "Your father liked pork," she says, with a look of nostalgia and mild confusion.

Into the cart we put peanut brittle, cookies with a dot of strawberry jam in the middle, a bag of jelly beans, an Oh Henry chocolate bar. These are the things Mother wants. At home, she eats very little. She can't finish dinner, but she always says, What is there for dessert? I have to have something sweet with my tea. Her day builds up into this little hill with something sweet on the top. Outside of sugar, she is not interested in food. She says she can't taste anything, she is never hungry. It is as though her body were dormant, as though all her bodily functions have come to a halt. She does not perspire anymore, she does not menstruate, she doesn't get up in the night to relieve herself.

In the fresh produce section, she stops, her feet planted firmly beneath her. "It was here," she says, pointing to the floor, "that he died. That is where he fell down." She is talking about a boy named Wally, with whom I went to grade school and who once had a crush on me.

"I know, Mother," I say.

"Dropped dead of an aneurism while he was hosing down the lettuce."

"Yes, Mother."

"Twenty-five years old. A bright boy. Wife and child. Terrible."

I try to move her along but she won't budge. She is suddenly strong enough, excited enough to resist me. It is as though her feet are rooted in the cement floor. We are standing beside a freestanding bin full of root vegetables. People have to steer their carts around us. One of the clerks passes in his white coat and smiles at us, curious and amused. I turn and feign interest in the turnips, running my palm over their thick, waxy surfaces.

"He should have married *you*," Mother tells me angrily. In recent years, her face has gotten yellow as a Chinaman's. Her teeth are brown with tea stains.

"Mother," I say a little impatiently, "he didn't look at me after grade four."

"Well, he *should* have."

"Let's get some ice cream," I say.

It is late on a wet, dark October afternoon and I am counting supplies at a large window in the back room of the dentist's office where I work as an assistant. The office is downtown, just off Main Street, in an old brick Victorian rowhouse with white gables and white spindle porch rails. It is a cozy office, with crooked walls and modern, muted lighting and many small, impractical examination rooms and soft music and grey silencing broadloom on the floors.

It is 5:15 and Dr. Peter Beveridge steps into the room and comes up behind me. "Everyone's gone home," he tells me. I myself have heard the last of the staff preparing to leave, the singing of coat hangers on the cloakroom rod, the hum of the evening traffic flowing in through the front door as it is opened again and again. *Goodnight, goodnight.*

Dr. Peter Beveridge places his hands on my hips.

"I want you to leave Mrs. Beveridge," I say without turning around. We are reflected together in the windowpane. He is a foot taller than I and brilliant as light in his white smock. He has been to Mexico and his face is bronzed and healthy. I look at his reflection and shake with desire and loathing. For three years I have worshipped him like a god: his height, his square, clean jaw, his moist, brown eyes, his slender hips, his tight backside, his smooth, perfect hair, his almost-military neatness.

"Oh, Jean," he says gently but firmly. He is fifteen years older than I and sometimes talks to me as though he were my father. "You feel depressed today," he tells me. "It's just the rain." We are looking out the window at the bank parking lot next door, where a diagonal rain is falling and the wind has flattened huge orange leaves against a wire fence.

"It's not the rain," I say angrily. Cars come and go in the parking lot. People run in and out of the bank, their collars turned up against the weather. Through the enormous plate glass windows of the bank I can see the customers lined up between crimson ropes, moving forward to the tall counters in the bright yellow light shining down from the lofty ceiling, talking to the tellers, carrying on their ordinary, innocent transactions, ready to run out again to their cars and go home, cook dinner, spend the evening with their husbands and wives and children. That is all I want, I think. A normal life.

If I let him, Dr. Beveridge will lead me out to reception, where there are warm lights and a long couch and a large aquarium in which jewel-coloured fish, gliding slowly through water, have a tranquillizing effect on patients, especially those coming to us for extractions, fillings, crowns. He will lay me down on the couch and make love to me with the fishes swimming by. Soon I will find that I am not thinking about him or feeling what is happening. I am not connected to him or to myself at all. I am watching the fish, enjoying their shapes and colours, the blacks, oranges, yellows, purples, fluorescent blues. It is easier to think about them than about what is going on. They regard me with rubbery, immobile eyes. They sway and turn and press their flat lips against the glass. They blow bubbles at me. I feel sorry for them in their watery prison. I am numbed by their slow, perpetual motion.

Dr. Beveridge says that he is sick. He is sick of dentistry. He wants to spend the balance of his life duck hunting. He is sick of toothrot and halitosis and cash flow and mortgages. He is sick of his beautiful wife. She is too good, too perfect. She makes life seem intolerable.

Sometimes she comes into the office wearing her simple, expensive clothes: wool slacks, a blazer, a thick, cream-coloured turtleneck sweater, loafers. I cannot stop looking at her clear, olive skin, her deep dimples, her large dark eyes, her cap of straight, shiny, hair. She is like a beautiful doe – serene, graceful, harmless.

One evening in September, Dr. Beveridge calls me at home. He never calls me there and I can tell that his wife must be standing at his elbow because he speaks in a formal way. Would I consider babysitting for them that evening? It is asking a lot, he acknowledges, it is very short notice, he is afraid I might have some social thing of my own to go to (here, he is being – something. cute? ironic? unkind?). Their scheduled babysitter has cancelled on them and there is a function they must attend. I would be doing them a great favour.

I eat an early dinner with Mother and then walk over through the darkness to their house. I am excited about seeing Dr. Beveridge on a weekend night, excited about getting a look at the inside of his house for the first time, and about being near him when his wife is there. I feel nervous and hypocritical and aroused and ashamed. I am too dressed-up for babysitting, having put on a silk blouse, short skirt, black nylons, black suede high heels. One of his sons (age ten) answers the door and then his wife comes forward with her beautiful white smile and her kind, trusting face.

"Oh, Jean," she says, taking my hand warmly. "This is so good of you." She is plainly dressed, in low pumps, a simple black wool crepe dress, small pearl earrings, but I have never seen anyone look more gorgeous with such little effort. Her beauty is so pure and true and natural and sustaining, like clear spring water or plain white bread.

The house, a long, low bungalow, is just as I've expected it to be – unpretentious but elegant. Low, pearly light, champagne broadloom, white leather couches, long expanses of sheer-draped window. Serenity. Silence like a cocoon, all sound absorbed by the deep carpet and the raw-silk wallpaper.

Mrs. Beveridge leads me into the livingroom, where there are many people standing in little groups, drinking cocktails and eating fancy bits of food before they all go out together to this important dinner.

"Everybody!" she says, calling their attention to me. "This is Jean, Peter's assistant. She's saved our lives tonight. She's staying with the boys."

They all turn to me then, in their silk dresses and dark suits and ruffled shirts and bow ties. They look at my inappropriate clothes and smile coldly at me as if to say, Well, if she's the babysitter, what's she doing in here with *us*? Then Dr. Beveridge says, "Come on, I'll show you the boys' rooms. This way."

I precede him down a long, carpeted hallway. We never reach the boys' rooms because he pushes me into the master bed-room and swiftly, silently pulls the door closed behind us. He calls me a beautiful bitch, though I am not beautiful at all, I am homely. Maybe the bitch part is true, though. He tears at my blouse. I watch a button fly across the room. He bites my neck, my shoulders, my breasts and while he is doing this, I am look-ing around, cataloguing the contents of the bedroom, observing Mrs. Beveridge's hairbrush and face cream on the dresser, her jeans lying across a sweet upholstered chair that looks like it is meant for a doll's house, the closet doors standing open and her clothes hanging there beside his, the soft track lighting, the thick pocket novel lying open on the low, wide waterbed. Then he straightens his tie in the mirror and goes back to his friends, leaving the door slightly ajar. Their ugly laughter drifts in to me as I crawl across the carpet looking for my button and flap-ping my blouse to dry his slobber off it so I can go out and find the boys' rooms for myself.

When I am putting him to bed, Eric, the son who answered the door says, "Do you work for my father?" He is a serious, fair boy with a round, gourd-like head.

"Yes," I answer. "I'm his dental assistant."

"What do you do?"

"I keep the examination room organized. I hand him whatever instruments he needs to work with. I mix up the substances he uses in the patients' mouths."

"That sounds boring."

"It's not boring," I say, cool but defensive. "It's interesting. You have to be very organized. You have to be quite intelligent to be a dental assistant."

"You don't *look* intelligent," he says.

It is late one evening when I leave the office. The rush hour traffic has subsided, people are in their houses, eating dinner. I walk home through the dark, quiet, leaf-strewn streets, looking at all the bright windows in people's homes and the shadows of figures moving behind drawn curtains. Presently, I come to Mother's grocery store, which is closed for the evening but fully lit inside, with strong yellow light. I am passing the store when I notice a solitary figure in a long white smock working in the produce section, stacking heads of lettuce in a deep bin. I pause and approach the window because I think I recognize – yes, I recognize Wally, his tall, tense figure, his swift movements, his jet-black hair, his square, earnest jaw, the peculiar frypan flatness of the back of his head.

The year he came to our school, he chased me every recess in the yard and pinned me against the red brick wall of the school, breathing hard in my face. I could have escaped him. I could have run faster to begin with, or, once he'd caught me, I could easily have slipped out from under his arms, but I chose to stay there, pressed against the rough bricks, with his breath on me. I wanted to look up at his clean, sharp face and his dark, troubled eyes. The next year, his father, who drove the town fire-truck, miscalculated a corner and ploughed into a bank wall, killing himself. Then Wally forgot all about me.

I linger now outside the grocery store and wait. Finally, Wally turns and sees me standing under a streetlamp with the empty light behind me and the wind bending the tall, thick pines enclosing the illuminated grocery store parking lot across the street. His eyes are large and blank and drained of all hope and passion. They say to me, I know who you are and I know who I am and it doesn't matter. Nothing matters because I am going to die young and possibly I have known all my life that I am going to die young and maybe it is a good thing because I wanted to be a news broadcaster but here I am in a seedy grocery store tending vegetables. He turns and wheels the empty trolley to the back of the store, where he disappears through great swinging aluminum doors.

Dr. Beveridge says to me, "Jean, you're driving me crazy," because I have told him, "Keep your hands off of me. If you touch me I'll scream at the top of my lungs. I mean it."

"Jean, don't do this to me," he says.

"Leave her and you can have me again," I say.

"I am the hunter and you are a little purple-winged duck," he used to tell me, and he'd pursue me all day long. Little pinches and strokes as I squeezed past him in the examination room. Nicks and bites between patients. Mouth against my neck. Finger down my collar. Hot breath in my hair. Fingers up the sleeve of my uniform at the x-ray station. A hand down my front in the supply room. In the empty staff room, a hand shooting, swift as an arrow, up under my skirt and inside my panties. And I was supposed to keep working, I was not to flinch or jump or shiver or indicate in any way my excitement. I was to go on mixing up the platinum in a little dish, sliding the tiny x-rays into their sleeves, arranging the gleaming instruments in the notches around the circular tray, fastening the paper bibs around the patients' necks, as though nothing had happened. That was part of the game. There was this buildup, this mounting of desire, all day long, until the office emptied out and we were alone.

"I want to be something more important to you than a game," I tell Dr. Beveridge. "I'm tired of being your toy."

"You're not my toy, Jean," he says sadly, shaking his head.

He tries to carry on. Leaning over his patients, his fingers in their mouths, he pauses and looks across their foreheads, searching my face. I sit on a high stool, with my feet resting on a rung. I lay an instrument firmly in his extended hand and in the instant before I can let go, we connect, there is an electric charge, a current running between us, through the innocent metal probe, with its sharp, delicately curved tip. I feel the power of his grip, the maturity and intelligence of it, the maleness that set my heart pounding the first time I assisted him. I try not to look at his immaculate hands and square, manicured nails, I try not to watch his beautiful fingers, which are long and white and graceful as a pianist's. I catch him staring at my knees. A fine perspiration forms on his upper lip. His hands begin to shake.

"Jean, you're going to ruin me," he says after the patient has left the room.

One night after work, he catches my arm in the hallway. "Jean, you're acting like I don't exist," he hisses.

"You don't," I say, pulling on my coat. I have been making a point of leaving with everyone else, so that he cannot corner me. I run out into the night with the others, clattering down the wooden porch steps, and hear my own voice, shrill, sad and gay, calling, too loud, to them, *See you tomorrow!*

One evening Dr. Beveridge says to me, "All right, Jean, you've won." He hands me a key. "I've rented a small apartment for us. We'll live there on a month-to-month basis until things settle down and we can find something more comfortable. I'm going home to tell Angela. You tell your family too. I'll meet you at the apartment at eight o'clock tonight."

Then he takes me out to reception and makes love to me again, in the blue quivering light of the aquarium. I am in rapture. I look up at the shining fish moving in their transparent, deadly regions. Suddenly I enter, I am transported into the aquarium's landscape of sunken ships and treasure chests and scuba divers. My body floats, is sucked into one of the black, watery caves. I close my eyes and the searing colours of the fish flash up against my eyelids. I feel the fish moving over me, wave after wave of them, their scaly, wafer-thin bodies brushing the length of mine like feathers.

It is late when I arrive home.

"Jean," Mother says, relieved to see me. "It's nearly seven.

We wondered." She and Floyd and Blanche are nearly finished dinner, which cannot be delayed on my account because Blanche gets hungry. I see that Mother has set aside something for me on a plate on the stove, with a lid on it.

"Too bad you came home," Blanche says, disappointed. "I was thinking of eating your dinner."

"Go ahead and eat it," I tell her indifferently. "I won't be sitting down."

"Jean," says Mother, detecting something in my face, "Is there anything wrong?" The three of them, their cutlery poised in the air, have stopped to observe me.

"She looks smug about something," says Blanche cautiously.

"You may as well know," I tell them, "that Dr. Beveridge and I have been carrying on an affair. He's leaving his wife tonight. We're meeting later this evening."

"I knew it!" exclaims Blanche, though her soft, pudding-like face is quivering with surprise. "Floyd, stop her. How will this look? She'll bring disgrace on us all."

Floyd's mouth is pinched with piety. "Jean, this is a terrible thing," he says.

"She's gone mad," Blanche says.

"Where will you go?" asks Mother. What she means is, *will you be warm? will you eat enough? will you have a comfortable bed?* When you get old, all you can give is an old woman's advice. All you can remember are the things your mother told you, which are the things her mother told her, which are the same things her mother told her before that. These are the absolutes. Dress for the weather. Don't stay up late. Wear shoes that fit. Nothing else can be known for sure. As for affairs of the heart, those foolish, futile, transitory pursuits, why even try to look for prescriptions, formulae?

"You can't just walk out like that," says Blanche. "It's not right."

"Father walked out," I remind her, "and nobody seems to blame *him* for it."

"That's different," Blanche answers. "He's a man. Men get

restless. There are things they have to work out of their systems."

"Oh, rot!" I say. "I've spent all my adult life doing the right thing, living here with Mother, supporting her when it was Father's job." At this, Mother blinks rapidly and presses her lips together. "Now I'm going to do something for myself," I say and I go upstairs, still wearing my coat. Floyd comes up after me, followed soon by Blanche, who lurks on the landing, thinking I didn't hear her heaving herself up the steps. I feel her bulk on the other side of the door, like that of a large witless animal. Her breath whistles through her throat. Her small black eyes peer through the crack in the door.

"It's never too late to repent," Floyd tells me.

Ignoring him, I tear my clothes out of the closet. Hangers fly across the room. I pull things out of drawers and fling them into two suitcases.

"It won't last, Jean," Floyd says to me. "These things never do. He'll leave you eventually and all you'll be left with is your sin and your shame."

I let myself into the apartment with the key Dr. Beveridge gave me. I put my suitcases down and walk from room to room, turning on lights, observing the furniture, which is plain and threadbare and somewhat ugly. I sit down at the livingroom window, which overlooks the road, and wait. I glance at my watch. I get up and raise the heat on the thermostat. I walk around the rooms again, test the taps in the bathroom, browse through the kitchen cupboards, turn on the television. I sit down and wait some more. Again I look at my watch. I have been here nearly two hours. It is now past nine o'clock. Finally the phone rings and I grab for it.

"Jean," Dr. Beveridge's voice comes over the line. "It's me."

"I know that," I say. "Where are you?"

"I can't do it," he says.

"What do you mean?"

"I swear to God, I came home with every intention of carrying through. But, Jean, I came in and dinner was ready. They'd held it up for me. Angela had cooked a roast and the boys were full of news about their hockey club. Everyone was so beautiful and excited. Everyone was so happy. I couldn't spoil it."

"Tell them tomorrow night, then," I say, noticing that I've begun to shake. "I've waited three years. I can wait a little longer."

"You don't understand, Jean," he says, his voice growing firmer. "Basically, we *are* a happy family. I'm not coming over there. I'm calling it off."

"Maybe you don't understand, either," I tell him. "I've made the break with my family. I'm waiting here for you."

"They'll get over it," he says. "Nobody else has to know. Tell them not to tell anybody else."

"You have humiliated me," I say.

"Jean," he says. "You can't come back to the office. I'm letting you go. I'll have your outstanding wages and your severance pay mailed to you tomorrow. I'll write you a letter of reference, if you want. I'm not worried about you. You're a good assistant. You won't have any trouble finding another job. And Jean, don't make trouble. It'll only backfire on you somehow. Let things go. Forget about it all. Accept it and move on. Don't let yourself get bitter."

I crawl into bed in my clothes and sleep all the next day and the next. When I finally get up, snow is falling. It is December, after all. I put on my housecoat and a pair of thick wool socks and sit at the livingroom window for two more days. Big, soft, independent flakes come down. I watch them in all their calmness, in all their individuality and separateness, and this seems to give me strength. At first, they melt, these beautiful snowflakes, when they touch the ground and this brings me a sense of peace. I feel myself melting, dying with them as they fade into the warm gardens, the still green grass. Gradually, though, they build up, coating lawns, roofs, driveways. The apartment is on a wide, busy residential street. From my window, I watch pedestrians tramping over the white sidewalks, cars creeping through the flying snow, crowded buses with wipers, long as a man's arm, beating back and forth. I have the sensation of watching the world from a great, wise height.

I go out and get groceries. I eat scrambled eggs, jello, raisin pie. I have a lot of time to think. I go out for walks and find myself picking my way down a small slope to the Lion's Pool, which is closed, of course, for the winter. I stand outside the high wire fence. Snow is falling in the pool where Floyd and I once swam and dove into the blue water, shrieking. All the children shouting. I hear their happy cries echoing against the low yellow brick wall. I smell the dankness of the change rooms and remember splashing through the shallow chlorine bath on my way out to the pool.

Snow is falling too, on the bleachers, where there were always a few parents scattered, waiting patiently for their children. I see Mother among them, her face bent to her book, in the days long ago when she could read fine print. Now she has only peripheral vision. There is a big black hole in the centre of everything she looks at. I have begun to think that this condition has affected her intellectual perceptions. She doesn't see the centre of things. She doesn't see the issues. She sees only the things surrounding them.

I think about how I used to come in the front door after work and find Mother sitting at the kitchen table with her hands lightly folded on her lap, waiting patiently for me to come home, her face full of calmness and hope. Just from her pose, I knew that she thought about me all day long. She never left the house. She moved from room to room, dressing slowly, looking out the windows, picking up her novel, in which she progressed slowly, sometimes reading the same page over and over again, forgetting she'd already read it, glancing now and then at the clock, thinking: Jean will be having lunch now. Jean will be cleaning up. Jean will be home in an hour. The thought of her tranquillity, her vigilance, used to sustain me.

One day I call home.

"Winter is here again, Mother," I say.

"Hello, Jean," she says. "Yes, I know."

"I have to find another job, Mother."

"That's fine, Jean," she says. "You'll find one."

"I never meant that," I tell her, "about supporting you. You know I like living with you."

"I know you didn't," she says, and begins to cry. "I'm just so happy to hear your voice," she says.

"You knew about Dr. Beveridge and me, didn't you?" I say.

"No, I didn't know. How would I know?" she says cautiously.

"You knew, Mother. You knew and you never said anything. Say you knew. I can't come home unless you admit it."

"Yes, I knew," she says. "It upset me but I could see it was helping you. You aren't a happy person, Jean."

For a moment neither of us speaks. We listen patiently to the silence, are comfortable with it. I can feel her physical presence at the other end of the line.

"Mother?" I finally say.

"Yes?"

"Why aren't you angry with Father?"

"He must have had his reasons for leaving, Jean," she says, "and some day he'll come home and explain them to me."

I won't go so far as to say I missed Floyd and Blanche in the few weeks I lived in the apartment. But when I move home I find them easier to accept. I seem to have a new appreciation for them and even catch myself listening for the sound of their footsteps coming in through the front door at dinnertime or on the weekends, though I would never admit it to Mother. At Christmas, Floyd says, "Jean, come with us to church, just this once," and I do. Then it becomes a habit. What else is there to do with Sunday mornings? I learn to pray and I learn to forgive. I forgive Father for not taking us to Florida with him and I forgive Dr. Beveridge for living on with his wife and his two gourd-headed boys in the beautiful bungalow on the nice curved street.

On Sunday mornings, we return from church in Floyd's car, Mother and I sitting in the back, Blanche in the front, flowing jelly across the bench seat.

"I prayed for Father this morning," Blanche tells us over her shoulder.

"I prayed for Jean," says Floyd.

"I prayed that Floyd will be sent to the African missions, where he'll be eaten by cannibals," I say.

"Oh, Jean," says mother, shocked and amused, "you don't mean that!"

"Of course I do."

In the evenings, Mother and I watch television.

"Can you see from where you're sitting?" I ask her.

"Yes, I can see," she says. "I can see everything." She is afraid of being perceived as infirm. She is afraid of being shoved away in a seniors' home.

"Are you sure?" I say. "Do you think you should move closer? Why don't you sit in this chair?"

"No, no," she says, "don't worry about me. I'm fine."

And I know it is all darkness.

ANNE CARSON

Water Margins: An Essay on Swimming by My Brother

It is like water whose nature remains the same. But as gods, human beings, hungry ghosts and fish do not carry the same effect forward from past causation, they each see water differently. Gods see it as jewels, people in the world see it as water, hungry ghosts see it as pus and blood and fish see it as a palace.
– anonymous 5th century commentary on
   the *Treatise On Emerging Awake*

PREFACE

> *Brother (noun) associate, blood brother, cadet, colleague,*
> *fellow, frater, frere, friar, kinsman, sibling, soul brother,*
> *twin brother, See* CLERGY, FRIEND, KINSHIP.
>   *– Roget*

My brother once showed me a piece of quartz that contained, he said, some trapped water older than all the seas in our world. He held it up to my ear. *Listen,* he said, *life and no escape.*

This was a favourite phrase of his at that time. He had dropped out of high school to do martial arts and his master liked to say "life and no escape" when translating the Chinese word *qi*, which means breath or energy and is fundamental to good kicks. I remember we were down by the lake, it was sunset, fireboat clouds were lining up on the horizon. He was doing his Mountain Movements Sea Movements exercises. *Pervasive but you can't see it physical but has no body.* His left foot flashed past my head. *Qi is like water, the master says, we float on the water when the level is right everything swims.* His right foot cut the air to ribbons. *Put it in your mind you've got a wishing jewel.* It was cold sitting there in the November wind but I liked being with him. We had survived a lot together. It's true he hated me all through childhood – for my ugliness, he had explained simply, and this seemed reasonable enough. But around the age of fourteen hatred gave way to unexpected days of truce, perhaps because I caught up to him in school and was affable about doing his homework. Who cares why. A sun came out on my life. We spent a lot of time that winter driving around town in his truck listening to the radio and talking about Dad or sex. Well, he talked.

His stories were all about bad luck. It wasn't his fault that headlights got smashed, the school flunked him, his girlfriend thought she was pregnant, the police arrested him for driving naked on the beach. But good luck, he felt, was just around the corner. He was someone bound for happiness and he knew where to find it. He knew he was close. Very close. As I listened to him a sadness began in me that I have never quite put down. Still, it pleased me that he thought I was smart and asked my opinions about things. He called me Professor and gave me *Roget's Thesaurus* in the deluxe two-volume edition for Christmas. It is here beside me, volume one at least. He never got around to giving me volume two.

For some reason he believed in me. *She's going to be someone you know*, he said to my mother once. I heard this from her only after he was gone. It was late spring when he disappeared, for reasons having partly to do with the police, partly with my father, it doesn't matter now. Postcards came to us from farther and farther away, Vermont, Belgium, Crete, with long spaces of time in-between them. No return address. Then very early one morning, about three years after he left, he called from Copenhagen (collect). I stood on the cold linoleum, listening to a voice that sounded like him in a padded costume. Layers and layers of hard times and resentment crusted on it. He had got his front teeth knocked out in a fight and needed a large sum for dentistry. He asked me to send money and not tell Dad. After he hung up it took several moments to unclench my fingers from the telephone.

A card came from Copenhagen after I wired the money. He was on his way east, heading for China. Cards came from Paris and then from Marseille – I remember that one, it was his birthday and he was buying drinks for everyone in the bar. A card came from Israel, rather sadder. A card came from Goa, mentioning heat and dirt and the monsoon delayed. Then no more cards came.

I don't reckon my brother ever got to China. So I made him a wishing jewel.

FRIDAY 4 A.M.   NOT SWIMMING.

Black motionless night. Bushes. The swimmer stands at the window. Ducks are awake down by the water's edge.

FRIDAY 4 P.M.   SWIMMING.

In late afternoon the lake is shaded. There is the sudden luxury of the places where the cold springs come flooding up around the swimmer's body from below like an opening dark green geranium of ice. Marble hands drift enormously in front of his face. He watches them move past him down into the lower water where red stalks float in dust. A sudden thin shaft of fish smell. No sleep here, the swimmer thinks as he shoots along through the utterly silent razorglass dimness. One drop of water entirely awake.

SATURDAY 6.30 A.M.   SWIMMING.

At dawn a small mist cool as pearls hangs above the lake. The water is dark and waits in its motionless kingdoms. Bars of light proceed diagonally in front of the swimmer as he moves forward following the motions of the strange white hands. Gold rungs slide past beneath. Red water plants waver up from the bottom in an attitude of plumes. How slow is the slow trance of wisdom, which the swimmer swims into.

SATURDAY 9 A.M.   SWIMMING.

The swimmer prowls among the water lilies at the water's edge. Each has a different smell (orange, honey, milk, rot, clove, coin) like people. He is putting his nose into one calyx after another, wondering if they compete for him when an insect of the type called a darning needle rows into his eyelashes. Rival suitor. The swimmer backpaddles and moves hugely on his way, through underwater courts of brides swaying the wonderful red feathers of their legs as lengths of visible secret. The water mounts pleasures at him through every doorway. Exposed. He swims off.

Pingliang Monastery
Pingliang

*well I see a little cloud of dust coming along the road maybe
it's you no in answer to your question God has not forbidden
me the use of the mails* WHO? *as to your letters I cherish your
letters I buy everyone a drink and read them aloud yes the
monks appreciate such things I taught them the phrase "happy
hour"* HUNG IT ON A COW'S HORN *well it's true I'm no scholar
and as you point out don't even know Chinese but I like to see
how things work once I saw a poem called Taro Moon it had
seventeen characters the seventeenth is the moon because the
moon rises above mountains in the east at the end of the poem
letting its whiteness fall through the night on the other characters an old man and a boy washing taro roots by the riverside
scrubbing away with poles in a bucket you see taro roots are to
be offered to the harvest moon on the fifteenth day of the
eighth month – but look there is the moon already risen in the
eighth character! very bright on the taros No use plaiting a
rope after the thief is captured say the characters in-between
what kind of rebuke is this? no one understands it meanwhile
my advice to you is get a girlfriend you'll be old soon you're
already weird start work on this today we're praying hard* YOU
KILLED MY COW

TUESDAY 2 P.M.   SWIMMING.

Afternoon banked over with white clouds. The water darkens to greenish black. Nothing visible in it except its own bottomlessness. The swimmer's hands move in front of his face like two pieces of early winter. Forty-year-old knuckles square as a carpenter's in Chekov. When he was young forty had seemed a magical age. He had imagined himself holding a cigarette in his long white fingers, conversing wryly with women who leaned towards him. Now he wonders what eighty-year-old hands will look like, their strange marble kindling the black water before him. Perhaps it is time – a detached red stalk brushes the side of his face like something alive.

Pingliang Monastery
Pingliang

well as long as I'm studying my heart out up here how about a
few facts you like facts the nature of the mind is identical with
empty space when it meets the wind waves appear am I right?
Pingliang Mountain 7,533 feet high situated between the nar-
rowing easternmost boundaries of Hoh Xil Hu province is
sparsely vegetated with eucalyptus desert pine thyme trees
and azaleas which flower even in the snowfields above the
treeline because yes the spirit of God is loose in them
Pingliang Mountain Monastery built in A.D. 1300 by the
Pingliang master (Qi Miao) whose name means DON'T FOR-
GET THE MIDNIGHT THOUGHT *stands in its own light on a*
northern slope on cold stones Right at this moment, what is it
like? said a young girl (sent to test his purity) there she was
embracing old hermit Qi Miao and he said Like waking up in
the night to find the hermitage burnt down (he failed the test)
this is your brother the Leave Home Person the Wisdom Crane
the Boy Of Rock the Ten Fields Of Happiness saying "CHARLES
BUKOWSKI SAYS THERE MUST BE SOME WAY WE HAVEN'T
THOUGHT OF YET"

SUNDAY 8 A.M.   SWIMMING.

A Sunday flood of hot light pounds down onto the black glass of the lake. The swimmer is grateful to escape underneath to where his dim water kingdom receives him. Silently. Its single huge gold nod. Who else ever knew me, the swimmer thinks. The hand with the wedding ring floats down past his face and disappears. No one.

Pingliang Monastery
Pingliang

*of course you're depressed you haven't had a girlfriend in three
years am I right? remember your wedding day we were in the
taxi in traffic I said So you think she'll stay with you? you just
looked at me* THE MIND OF ANY MAN MAY AT ANY MOMENT
AND IN ANY PLACE SINK INTO HELL *(Qi Miao) well that's
enough compassion let's get on to facts the Linji school of
Buddhism has a multi-observational practice involving relentless investigation of kong-ans during meditation while the
Caodong school practices non-observational meditation (also
called silent illumination) a method for calming one's mind
without trying to solve any question when Qi Miao at one
time became ill due to the rigours of his multi-observational
practice the healer advised him to try non-observation for
awhile well he couldn't it being against his tradition also he
saw the monks in the hall asleep during group practice so
silent was their illumination I'm somewhat horrified he confided so the healer gave him another method this was to
suppose a lump of cream exquisitely yellow-white smooth
moon-sweet was placed on his head gradually coming
down together with his mind spreading throughout his whole
body Qi Miao returned home practiced cream-observation
before three years he was cured and solving some challenging
kong-ans besides this is your brother the Gateless Gate the
Hardbottomed Bag the Lake On Fire reminding you there is
neither one nor many there is only* SUCH *please remember I
love you it's not a window* IT IS THE VIEW

THURSDAY 12 P.M.   SWIMMING.

At noon the water is a cool bowl where the swimmer drops and darts away from the broiling air. He aligns himself and moves forward with his face in the water staring down at the bottom of the lake. Old beautiful shadows are wavering steadily across it. He angles his body and looks up at the sky. Old beautiful clouds are wavering steadily across it. The swimmer thinks about symmetries, then rotates himself to swim on his back staring at the sky. Could we be exactly wrong about such things as, he rotates again, which way is up? The swimmer swims slowly watching shadows shaped like camels and noses and Japan flow on without pause. High above him he can feel the clouds watching his back, waiting for him to fall towards them.

THURSDAY 5 P.M.   SWIMMING.

The swimmer lets himself fall out of the day heat and down through a gold bath of light deepening and cooling into thousands of evenings, thousands of Augusts, thousands of human sleeps. He is thinking of the light that sinks about her face in Leonardo's painting called The Virgin Of The Rocks. Once he saw her kneeling by the water. Now he plunges along through the cold rock colours of the lake. Haloes are coursing over the ridged mud of the bottom. He dives to get one. *If ever I forget my deep bond to you.*

Pingliang Monastery
Pingliang

*so if you loved her why did you throw her out or am I being
simple? consider how the fox catches bustards it droops its
head downward and gently wags its tail well I like your
abjectness I always liked it she liked it Father liked it everybody liked it but be careful of that mirror* WHY DOES NO DUST
ALIGHT ON IT? *if love unbalances you (and love unbalances
everyone) there are several things you can do some (staying
home from work to watch her) better than others (tying her to
the stove) but in general I don't think love likes force or being
forced into the headlights and stared at until it does something wrong What am I stealing from you? I heard her ask once
she had good questions this is your brother the Gaptoothed
Freedom Morning the Cart Shaft Pointing North the Blackbird
Never Before noting that most humans beat love to death
why? answer this and I'll tell you about the two parts of
wisdom* 1. NOT 2. SOUP

MONDAY 5.30 A.M.   SWIMMING.

Blue peaches are floating down onto the lake from under dawn cloud. The swimmer parts the water like a dancer peeling a leotard down her long opal leg. Sullen where he moves through its unlit depths – a smell of gasoline makes him stop and look round. A small silent rowboat is passing, two women in fishing hats studying him. Old ballerinas, he decides abruptly and dives out of sight.

MONDAY 12 P.M.   SWIMMING.

Noon darkness clamps down on the lake. The water feels black enough to dye his skin. Its cold pressure. A strange greening on top of the water. The swimmer is trying to remember a sentence from Rilke about the world one beat before a thunderstorm –

MONDAY 6 P.M.   SWIMMING.

Rain continues. The far hills are gun-coloured with ancient mist floating whitely before them. Chilly and concentrating hard the swimmer moves along just under the surface of the water, watching each drop hit the surface and bounce. Ping. Water on water. He is wondering how it would feel to be a voice in a mediaeval motet, not a person singing but a voice itself, all the liquors raining and unraining around it. Ping. Or to be a cold willow girl in the ancient hermit's embrace. High above him at the top of the sky blood clouds are gathering like a wound behind flesh.

MONDAY 10 P.M.   NOT SWIMMING.

Standing at the window the swimmer stares out through a stretching pitch-black wind towards the lake. He can feel it lift and turn like a sleeper in the same bed. Can hear the wind touch each link of its dreams in-between. What does a lake dream? Ping.

Pingliang Monastery
Pingliang

*our vows include the idea that no one's enlightenment can be
considered complete as long as any suffering being remains in
the world this is your brother the Buddhist Tracer Bullet telling you YOU'RE STUCK I've seen you sit in your kitchen watching the phone ring tears running down your face yes I agree
there are some things humans can't help each other with but
remember the night Father showed us how to look at stars? we
had the telescope in the driveway Don't point it straight at
where you want to see he said Look a little to the left you
know it's like Qi Miao how he yearned for the holy land of
China so he sailed and began to walk there he was traversing
moving sands and steep ridges there he was using scaling lad-
ders to connect precipices when the cold moon flooded down
he thought This journey is endless when his teachers spoke he
did not feel the white mist lift from his eyes finally he began a
hundred-day retreat on Won Gak The Mountain Of Now Or
Never a continuous diet of pine needles beaten into powder
combined with ice-basin baths and twenty hours daily meditation produced some very strong doubts in Qi Miao there he
was packing his bag there he was travelling down the mountain his heart like a hailstorm he stopped to ask for water at
the hut of an old woman she said No he said What? she said
No he said Please she knocked him down with her broom Qi
Miao sprang up shouting YOU STUPID CUNT all at once everything became lucid he stayed with her seven months and
learned to make an ink brush out of a badger's tail*

FRIDAY 4 A.M.   NOT SWIMMING.

Staring. The lake lies like a silver tongue in a black mouth.

FRIDAY 8 A.M.   SWIMMING.

The storm has cleared. A blinding gold wind knocks hard waves flat across the swimmer's face as he plunges forward, trying to place himself in the trough of it but the diagonals shift and mock him. On the surface the water is navy blue and corrugated by wind. Spots of white foam crowd hectically up and down the waves. There is an urgency to it as if a telephone were ringing in the house. But there is no telephone in the house.

FRIDAY 6 P.M.   SWIMMING.

A dark blue wind is driving sunset home. The swimmer glances from under his arm at the shoreline where poplar trees are roaring with light and dropping their leaves to silver in the wind. With each stroke of his arm the swimmer exchanges this din for the silence beneath, his sliding green kingdom of hungers, monotonies and empty penetrations. To open this treasury is not for one's father or brother or wife to decide. Oneself.

Pingliang Monastery
Pingliang

*yes since you ask I do find monastic life pretty straight Qi
Miao's rulebook Daily Tasks Each Person Must Know prescribes every aspect even down to the ritual for feeding the
hungry ghosts (the basic idea is to feed them truth) but you
know it cheers me to think of this man living in a time of
moral decay (1253-1333) history having withdrawn the blessing of truly charismatic teaching or breakthrough people and
who must have known he was a dull person not the type to
"stride into the tiger's cave to lay hold of a cub" yet there he
was writing away at his rule there he was trying to get things
clean for other people besides he had a girlfriend do you want
to hear one of the poems he wrote her*

> *STARS DO NOT MEET THEY WOULD EXPLODE*
> *AMONG HUMANS NO SUCH THING AS A CHANCE*
> *MEETING*
> *WE MAY BE UNAWARE OF THIS OURSELVES*
> *DOES A LANDSCAPE VANISH BECAUSE A BLIND MAN*
> *WALKS THROUGH IT?*

WEDNESDAY 8.30 A.M.   SWIMMING.

Small white bundles of mist are hurrying over the still surface of
the lake. I wonder why I don't dream anymore, the swimmer is
thinking as he inserts himself into the dark green glass. There
were times he used to dream a lot. Now the nights are blank,
except for intervals when he rises to look at the lake. And then
behind his back he can feel the cat wake and observe him from
its lit eyes. Not lifting its head. It is a very old cat (a gift from his
brother) and seems to be dying. Before they go back to sleep he
gives the cat to drink from a teacup of water in which he has
dissolved some drops of honey. It eats little solid food nowadays
but dreams well at night, so far as he can judge from its mutters
and tiny thrashings. What unaccountable longings and hidden
fears are swimming on fire in you? he wonders as he leans on
the bed in the dark watching the small fur body. Almost everything physiologists know about the living brain has been
learned from sleeping cats. Sleeping or waking, cat brains most
resemble human brains in design. Cat neurons fire as intensely
as human neurons, whether bombarded from without or from
within. Lightly, lightly he touches its head where the suffering
bones come haunting through old flesh. A glow enters his fingers, as if it were a pearl dreaming.

WEDNESDAY 5.45 P.M.   SWIMMING.

The lake is cool and rippled by an inattentive wind. The swimmer moves heavily through an oblique greenish gloom of
underwater sunset, thinking about his dull life. Wondering
why it doesn't bother him. It bothered everyone else including
his father who died, his brother who left the country and his
wife who married again. *Why don't you do something?* they
would say, *Call someone? What about Pons? What about
Yevgeny?* Don't you paint any more? The swimmer would
glance out at the lake lying like a blue thigh in the open gold
breeches of the noon sun and forget to answer. Only the cat
does not question his lack of events. Where there is nothing to
watch, it watches nothing. Perhaps I am the cat's dream, the
swimmer thinks, breaking the surface.

Pingliang Monastery
Pingliang

*no I don't dream much nowadays (we get up at 3) the last time
I dreamed was in jail the old baseball nightmare remember? it
started the year I was seven you used to sit on my chest and
sing when I was yelling tell me why did you always sing
Chestnuts Roasting On An Open Fire even in June or July? it
wasn't much of a dream anyway there was this baseball game
where all the players are made of shit and slide around
screaming angry a very angry dream I imagine Freud had
something to say about this Qi Miao says dreams are a mad-
man shrieking on a mountain top he hears the echo far below
races down to search for it in the valleys shrieks again climbs
up to search among the peaks this is the usual condition for
the world to wonder which is which (dreams* NOT *dreams)
you'll never know you can't even point to it you'll spend your
life washing reality back and forth from one tin pie plate to
another or you could just stop right now go down the road
make* SOUP *for somebody so do you want to hear the final
entry in Virginia Woolf's diary "And now with some pleasure I
see that it is seven and must cook dinner haddock and sausage
meat I think it is true that one gains a certain hold on sausage
and haddock by writing them down" yes it's true you can
write on a wall with a fish heart (it's the phosphorous) this is
your brother the Path Of Homelessness the Hall Of Fierce
Determination the Kettle Of No Presence saying tell me about
something besides swimming how's the cat?*

MONDAY 5 A.M.   NOT SWIMMING.

Watching from the window. When they are brand new ballet shoes have this same sheen of pink and silver, as a lake glinting deep in the fringe of its leaves just before dawn. The cat stirs and groans. Behind its tight shut eyes millions of neurons are firing across the visual cortex. The swimmer bends down. A low rustle of longing sinks from the cat's small open mouth. Neurophysiologists think dreams begin in the brainstem, a box of night perched above the spinal column that also regulates such primitive functions as body temperature and appetite. The swimmer imagines himself dropping into the silent black water of that primitive lake. Shocks of fire flash and die above his head. The cold paints him. All at once he realizes it is not up to him, whether he drowns. Or why.

Pingliang Monastery
Pingliang

*I'm glad you're painting again thanks for the picture of the cat
I put it up over my bed alongside* DO NOT PICK UP HITCH-
HIKERS PRISON FARM NEARBY *roadside memento of my last
day in America and a copy of Qi Miao's poem "I Hate Incense"
you're right the cat is looking many kalpas older than when I
last saw it that cat must be nineteen or twenty by now am I
right? well we're all slipping towards the rim* AFTER THE LONG
RAIN CLEAR TO THE WEST A LITTLE SONG AT SUNSET *is Qi
Miao's poem on old age or more precisely on his old-age practice of visiting brothels to prolong youth the old tart if the dis-
ciples saw him he'd say* DON'T TRUST YOUR MIND IT'S WILD
IT'S ALWAYS MOVING *or if they rebuked him* FIRST SET YOUR
BITTER FEET IN THE SWEET STEPS *always moving always moving that's right (kalpa: the period required for a celestial
woman to wear away a ten-mile cubic stone if she touches it
with her garments once every three years)*

FRIDAY 4 A.M.   NOT SWIMMING.

The lake is a narrow fume of white mist still as a sleeping face in its dark bowl of leaves. One star hangs above. There is silver from it falling directly into the swimmer's eye. He glances at the cat asleep on the bed like a pile of dropped twigs. Looks back at the lake.

FRIDAY 4.20 A.M.   SWIMMING.

As he approaches the water's edge through soaked grasses he sees the mist open. He stops. Poised before him in the bluing air is a kingfisher heron almost as tall as himself. It is staring out over the lake. As the swimmer watches without breathing, the kingfisher totters profoundly forward from one red leg to another, then all of a sudden gathers itself and in a single pensive motion vanishes through a hole in the mist. The hole closes. The swimmer stands a moment, then drops, down through the dark blue mirror of the lake, to search for red legs and balancings and memories of the way people use love – but the cat seems unawakened.

Pingliang Monastery
Pingliang

*so have you ever wondered why so many Buddhist anecdotes
are about shit? for example Qi Miao once travelled to Kai
Province to lecture on the phrase of truth* FORM IS NO DIFFER-
ENT FROM EMPTINESS *and found himself saying to the
assembled monks "a bowl of delicious soup is ruined by two
chunks of rat shit" well is it possible to get outside language
just you naked striking God in the face? not really so I'm making a collection of shit stories and otherwise spend the day
wandering up and down hills through wind craters like huge
bald babies remember the time we were driving across the
Mojave desert and saw the big yellow letters* I LOVE YOU
JOHNNY AND I DIDN'T DO ANYTHING *painted on a boulder?
you were reading aloud to me "heat feelings do not answer
specific moral dilemmas but may alter the relations between a
set of objects" from one of your phenomenology books Too bad
we can't get this news to Johnny I said and you started singing
Chestnuts Roasting On An Open Fire as loud as you could a
thousand white arms blew open on the sky like clouds*

SATURDAY 8 A.M.   NOT SWIMMING.

Robbed sentenced speechless. Bombarded like Socrates by voices of law from within, the swimmer awakens suddenly feeling like the wrong side of a wing flipped up in the wind. The morning sun is hitting him straight in the eye. From where he lies he can see the lake like a flat plane of gold. A hardworking blue Saturday wind pushing white cloud rags into their places on the sky. The cat is gone.

SATURDAY I P.M.   NOT SWIMMING.

A white eyelid of cloud has closed over the lake. The swimmer stands at the water's edge watching the surfaces of the water blacken and begin to move. Little starts of wind arrive from this direction and from that. Something is being loaded into the air from behind. The swimmer wonders about being struck by lightning. Who will feed the cat? Will his wife come to the funeral? Get hold of yourself, he thinks, but even in childhood he found Saturdays depressing, too porous, not like other days. He wonders where the cat has got to.

SATURDAY 3 P.M.   NOT SWIMMING.

No storm yet. The air has the pressure and colour of fresh-cut granite. Black lake surface is moving, keeps moving, slightly, all over. As if some deep underwater clocks were being wound slowly into position for a moment of revelry. *That she and I may grow old together.* The swimmer turns and goes back up toward the house.

SATURDAY 5 P.M.   NOT SWIMMING.

No storm no cat. The water stares.

Pingliang Monastery
Pingliang

in the high desert the light is clear as an alarm each object
exists in space on its own shadow of course there are also unat-
tached shadows which go roaming about sometimes con-
strued as ghosts they are just looking for an object Qi Miao
called them Stunt Riders there he was going on long treks fol-
lowing them up and down the peaks Are they male or female?
he wanted to know he had good Smell the rain? questions like
listening to a tap drip the moment it stops well you know what
a cheery guy I am generally but every year about this time I
withdraw for a while to a three-section reed hut above the
treeline it tends to be painful get ready this is your brother the
Radiant and Charming Month Of May the Grinding Of Bones
When Your Sleep Is Deep the Old Silver Kitchen Knife Of
Compassion saying FIGHT REALITY

THURSDAY 7.30 A.M.   SWIMMING.

White motionless mist and the steady screens of rain. A mediaeval city indicates itself ghostly on the opposite shore. The
swimmer stands at the water's edge, listens, feels his ears fill
with whiteness and time slip back a notch. He enters the water
and begins to swim, placing himself between the black breasts
of the water so that his stroke rolls him from wave to wave.
The shore moves past. A mountain comes into view. In
glimpses from under his arm the swimmer studies this
unknown mountain. He sees huge blue pine trees and soaked
rocks and white innards of mist hanging and trailing. From
between roots a bit of fire. Beside this fire some strange and
utterly simple soul keeping watch with its neck drawn into its
shoulders. Nipples darken the paper robe. Roasting horse
chestnuts and feeding them to something hunched on the log
by its side. When the swimmer gets back to the house he finds
the cat collapsed on the foot of the bed. Its wet fur smells vile.

THURSDAY 6 P.M.   SWIMMING.

The mist has slowed and deepened to one Chinese continuity
from lake to sky. Ragged darker areas mark the trees at the
water's edge. The swimmer has been moving steadily through
cold silver monotonies for some time. All of a sudden he stops
stroking and looks up. Glances around him through blurred
goggles. Unknown. What is that ringing sound? He pushes up
his goggles and peers. Nothing. No middle no edge. No ducks
no debts. Erased world. Over the whole water surface silence
comes aching at him. *Do your best, do your best,* can a man
vanish? He seems to be inside his own hearing. One plus two
equals zero. It is more than lost, there is nothing to be lost
from. Then all at once he sees them, far down the lake in the
wrong direction, the four Ophelias. Four white birch trees
(named for his wife) that mark the shoreline of his property. In
a black rush of joy he pulls down his goggles and sets off. *The
cat will mew,* said Hamlet standing in a grave and Ophelia said
By cock! Humans in love are terrible aren't they? Because

authentic desire is accessible to the mind alone and sexual activity, the notion that sexual activity is its aim, is a stupidity. He remembers lecturing his wife on this topic. *Alright call me stupid*, she had said slamming the door behind her. After the first year they led quite separate lives. He would watch her and wonder what it would be like to find his hunger answered in sex. *The surfaces of the body are a good place to start*, she said trying to be jolly, this was before she gave up. He studies her surfaces. He studied the various competing accounts of erotic desire. *We desire an entity whose mode of being differs radically from that of its media*, he read to her from a book, an *inescapably metaphysical problem*. She rested her chin on her hand. She bet him two dollars she could escape. Well who knows. For him it was like desiring colours. *Its object is nothing in this world. We cannot affect, except to destroy, it's instantaneous.* Desiring to eat them.

ascending
  Pingliang

well I'm on my way WHO IS IT WHO THROWS LIGHT *climbing Pingliang climbing up through the remains and devastation of the fires we had earlier this year I saw them burn as Chinese characters are written from left to right from top to bottom* ON THE MEETING OF THE MOUNTAINS? *climbing up through the black bubbled trunks of sequoias and desert pine that stand like lost souls some rising 200 feet in the air they do not sway in the wind they give no sound they have no shadows and in the cold sunset a curious ore soaks out of the ground* IS IT BECAUSE OF THE BRIGHTNESS IN MY HEART *so why do I think you need a girlfriend? well it depends what kind of reason you want when Americans began strip mining the southwestern hills of China two hundred years ago the Chinese said No because you are letting the breath out of the ground when his disciple drove a gimlet into his thigh so he could meditate all night Qi Miao laughed Because I have found a better way to stay awake notice here and elsewhere in his writings the word he uses for sexual intercourse is Cloud rain I guess that is my favourite reason* THAT DARKNESS BECOMES REAL DARKNESS?

MONDAY 9 A.M.   NOT SWIMMING.

Heavy grey quilts of cloud have lowered themselves over the lake and a hard west wind is chopping the water black and white. Even from where he stands at the window the swimmer can see foam piled in the reeds at the water's edge. There is a feeling of early autumn. He turns away. The cat is heaped, motionless, on the foot of the bed. Bending, the swimmer ever so lightly kisses the small bald patch in front of its ear – the cat is immediately and totally awake, without moving any part of its body except one eye. The eye glares at him. Fundamentally sweet-natured, the cat is ornery now due to pain everywhere. It is over a hundred years old in human terms. Even its fur hurts, so far as the swimmer can tell. *Mine ache t'think on't,* he whispers. The eye closes.

MONDAY 4.30 P.M.   SWIMMING.

A disconsolacy seeps out of the grey light and wanders on the grey water. Cold ripples in series move toward shore. Somewhere up the hill a chainsaw chews into the air then stops. Silence comes lapping back. Shivering like a child the swimmer wades into the water. Childhood is nice in some ways, he thinks. Someone to hold a big towel and wrap you when you come out is nice. As he strikes off along the shore, grey waves slapping his face, the swimmer thinks about his father holding out the big towel and bundling it around him and murmuring *Do your best, do your best* in his slightly wild way. The lake wind whipping at them.

ascending
  Pingliang

*the rocks are bald they sway in the noon wind like white fires
the sweat runs into my eyes no shadows no sound except the
rat scream wind slicing along an inside shelf of my mind you
know that sound when you are digging by the well and hit
stone* KRKKKKKKKKKKKK *remember the time Father was peering down the well dropped his glasses then refused to get a
new pair he said Already I was seeing too much and we had to
move everything in the kitchen to the very front of the shelves*
IT BREAKS THROUGH THE BLUE SKY *when it shines on objects
there is no hate no love it does not shine on sandalwood before
shit it is called The Everywhere Equal Light (say the masters)
do you want to know a secret I hate light I hate shit I hate
masters the day I was born God put his finger up my ass and
pushed* THERE *said God* NOW YOU WILL HAVE BITTERNESS
INSTEAD OF PEACE ALL YOUR LIFE SEE WHAT YOU CAN DO
WITH THAT

FRIDAY 8.45 A.M.   SWIMMING.

The lake is a cold lead pane. Clouds and trees look saddened or dark. But underneath the water an odd verdigris glow is soaking out from somewhere. The swimmer swims along through rooms mysteriously lit as an early Annunciation. Stillness rushes everywhere. It is awake. It knows him and it cares nothing – yet to be known is not nothing. Sometimes the cat will look up suddenly with its eyes like two holes that pin him. *The world where we live is a burning house,* the eyes say. The swimmer glides deeper, thinking about the difference between fullness and emptiness. A few times it happened when he sat in the audience watching her dance that his wife's eyes came to rest on him – empty. He saw right to the back of her head. Modigliani would paint out the iris, which seemed to him too intimate.

FRIDAY 10 P.M.   NOT SWIMMING.

Over the unmoving black body of the lake the moon dreams its gold dream of life, as if it were alone in the world and what dreamer is not?

Hut 1. Not 2. Soup
Pingliang

life above the treeline is blank as the inside of a wrist no sound
except the wind whining along your earbone like a mendicant
shock green lichens occur here and there Francis Bacon would
call them "pure departures from the nervous system" on his
little planet of numb noons I know he's one of your heroes but
that's ONE PAINTER I NEVER LIKED *I hate noon I hate every-*
thing that happens at noon verticality light heat leavetakings
Father would lift his teacup and tilt back his head for the last
swallow of tea with a little sharp knock of the teacup against
his front tooth I hate that sound he would be standing by the
table untying his tie reaching for his fedora tucking the paper
under his arm gone out the kitchen door down the long path to
the car why do people look so much more lonely from the
back? this is your brother the Pit Meditator the Mouthwound
In A Fedora the Fishtrap Without The Fish beginning to have
good questions too

WEDNESDAY 7 A.M.   SWIMMING.

Deep straight holy dawn is tossing colours into the bowl of the lake – red blue green gold – he can taste them. As he swims he is thinking about standing beside his father in church. He was six. Leaning against the side of his father's coat that smelled of cold outside air and cigarettes gave him a feeling like an elevator going up. He looked around at other coats, balanced on one foot for a while. There was a bump inside his shoe, he tested it with his toe for live teeth. Then his knees began to make interesting corduroy noises against one another, he was starting to accompany them with zipper sounds on the front of his jacket and a light thumping on the hymnals when his father reached down and found his hand and put an object firmly into it.

It was a little book. On each page was a story and a painting of a saint – nothing exceptional except for the colours. Red ochre royal night blue China black lead white poison green "yellow enough to be thrown out" (Kafka) – colours so true they fell out of the paintings into his eyes like food. They taunted him all the rest of the day from behind the greyed world. They rained through his mind all that night while he tried to sleep. The next book his father gave him confirmed his suspicion that colours were food and vision a concupiscence. It was a story about cats who got ready for winter by melting down different colours of candy and knitting it into mittens. There were tangy lime green mittens, very cool peppermint blue mittens, sweet raspberry red mittens, butterscotch mittens yellow as the sun and black licorice mittens so shiny he kept touching the page – but not with his tongue this was not allowed. Concupiscence as such was not a word he knew until many years later. One late spring night he was studying for final exams when his brother climbed in the kitchen window and emptied his pockets on the table. *Where have you been?* the swimmer asked. *India,* said his brother, *Look at these.* All over the table were raw chunks of colour – emerald green and sapphire and ruby red and ebony and even some dull bits of gold. His brother was a smuggler. *Importer,* his brother corrected with a smile. The gems were uncut and none had been polished yet they glowed with a power of life that made the swimmer want to eat them. This is the difference, he thought, between a stone and a precious stone. The larger workings of human greed began to make sense to him from that moment. And he gazed at his brother with compassion, like a rumour come true.

WEDNESDAY 7 P.M.   SWIMMING.

The evening recedes into sobriety like a Flemish landscape under darkening sky. Streaks of sunset light the lake erratically and slip toward silver when the clouds close. The swimmer is very cold and perceives that the cat is dreaming of eels, he can feel their long coils shuddering along his body as he moves through the eyeless water. He pays attention to the eels, they become a mountain. He considers the mountain, it clears of all internal noise and vibrates like a drop of crystal. Vibrating too he looks along his own cheekbones from the inside and sees the structure of all sentient being unfold very simply from there. *Woul't drink up eisel! Drink a crocodile!* His father used to quote *Hamlet* all the time. Suddenly profoundly bored he turns and hastens toward shore.

FRIDAY 6.30 A.M.   NOT SWIMMING.

The lake is closed in a white fist of fog. The swimmer dozes, wakes abruptly, dozes again. Then he lies watching sheets of rain come down over the lake and listening to the long hush of rain on the roof. He is thinking about his father whose salient traits were two: a love of the sound of rain on the roof and a talent for bad timing. His face is hot now remembering a discussion on women, the only one they ever had, that his father began on a railway station platform one late summer afternoon. They were waiting for the train that would take him back to school. He was thirteen. As it happened he knew about women. His brother had spent the summer reading aloud to him from some French novels with no punctuation they found on the bottom shelf in their father's room (along with a boxed edition of Japanese woodcuts). The melted dream sentences of those novels spread him open like white summer sun. There was a young girl whose brother had her shave off her pubic hair – *It is so painful growing back,* she complained. The swimmer had dwelt on this fact for some time. Meanwhile when the train arrived his father was staring at the sky and talking about inversion, as he called it. All aboard. Bustle of luggage. *Do your best, do your best.* The swimmer felt all of a sudden hopelessly angry. He longed to lean his head against this man. Instead he got quickly into the train and did not look back.

Hut 1. Not 2. Soup
Pingliang

well speaking of loneliness did I ever tell you about the BLACK
[HAWK] MOTEL *(bulbs for* HAWK *burned out) on highway 140
somewhere between Coarsegold and Fresno one hot still September night your brother the minor criminal celebrating his
fortieth birthday sitting across the bed from a woman he
thought he loved but it was going down a wrong track I don't
know sometimes you can't stop you just keep going down a
wrong track* DON'T TURN AWAY I CAN'T BREATHE WHEN YOU
TURN AWAY *it gets so mixed up when love is uneven but all
love is uneven* I LOVE YOU MORE THAN IS GOOD FOR ME *long
night ahead trucks rolling past dregs of wine and two
liverwurst sandwiches littered on top of the* TV *guts hard as a
rock eyes full of tears* I KNOW YOU HATE TEARS *trying to keep a
grip by thinking of sad people who made it anyway Keats
Charles Bukowski Margaret Mead Virgil and whoever it was
who scrawled on the wall above the toilet You Can Really
Only Steal From People Who Live Magically yes this three-
section hut is lonelier than* BLACK [HAWK] MOTEL *and here we
have your brother the Hook In Clear Water the Sum Of One
Plus Two Equals Zero the Lichen Of Non-Attachment wondering why I can never remember your birthday it's some time
this month am I right! sorry*

TUESDAY 6.30 A.M.   SWIMMING.

Rose milk of mist pours down the gold slats of dawn onto the lake. No motion on the glass. The whole blue sky painted on it and the dark green surrounding hills and every water reed along the shore and a late lone boneshank of moon. There stand the four Ophelias leaning over to stare at their own long white muscles in reflection. Toes out. But clarity isn't exactly "truth" is it? What clear phrases had fallen from her lips. A school of minnows darts past, each one mirrored perfectly on the surface of the facts. *Get a life of your own,* she had said more than once, *Don't hinge on me.* I am I am I am I am I am I – but the swimmer says nothing. Through the burning world he slips on.

FRIDAY II P.M.   SWIMMING.

The lake has been inked out. Bent gold moon splashed with cloud. Wide awake *Because,* as Thomas Hardy says, *if you stop a wedding guest on the way to a wedding you better have something more unusual to relate.* More unusual than what? The swimmer pulses along thinking about the difference between waves and water. There are no waves at night. They come into being early in the morning and stop when no one is dreaming of them, like the events of a life. But suppose you took away all the events of a life, what would remain there more unusual than any wedding guest's eye? Before the waves come into being, water is not non-existent. After the waves disappear, you watch. Watch. *The bubble is out* – is it? The human brain, estimated to contain 80 million nerve cells, each simultaneously communicating with upwards of 10,000 others and transmitting between 2 and 100 messages every second, day and night, waking or sleeping, dreaming or not, is one of the most complicated lakes in the universe. The swimmer swims staring straight ahead. Night pours out of his eyes. He is thinking of his father who died with his eyes open. Not unusual in itself. But the old man's eyes had been open for a year and a half, every second, day and night, waking or sleeping, dreaming or not? No one knew. A small stroke, the doctors thought. They spoke of neurotransmitters confused and the young science of defectology. Better not meddle, they decided – after all, permanently open is better than permanently closed isn't it? Is it? And so the swimmer sat beside the empty lake of his father on and off for a year and a half. He fed him and read to him and put drops in his eyes and watched him watch nothing. The old man never spoke, it was impossible to tell what he had heard. Does a lake dream? Then one night the swimmer, who had fallen into a reverie, looked up to find two eyes upon him groping over him like hands. It had grown dark in the room and emptiness was pouring out of the old man's eyes. And all of a sudden he grinned a deep cheerful *Do your best, do your best* grin and he was gone.

Hut 1. Not 2. Soup
Pingliang

night leaves clutch at blackness like anyone else I long to be
apprehended (loved) night is very long night is very long here
IS IT BECAUSE HE IS MAKING SUCH A FUSS rain drips from the
trees with a sound like many small human palms beating the
ground you know you can tell when the cat is dying first the
urinary tract breaks down then you'll see a white film come up
over its eyes from the bottom I am aware this does not answer
your question this is your brother No Great Vessel however a
practical person he knows gazelle pieces in the trees mean a
cheetah nearby he knows if you follow a python trail to the
end you find a python he knows you can tell a Tartar from a
Turk by whether he buttons his garment to the right or to the
left he knows the cerebellum is a small 3-lobed structure
behind the occipital lobe at the posterior part of the brain
sometimes visible through the eyes in moments of intense
muscular effort (e.g. a ballet dancer in a deep split en pointe)
but your questions he does not know Such things are the
waves on which we sail says Qi Miao but where am I sailing?
and where are my hopes? these childish sentences once set
down keep on their pitiful cries forever THAT HE DOES NOT SEE
THE TIGER DOZING UNDER HIS LEFT ARM!

About the Authors

Anne Carson is a professor of Classics at McGill University in Montreal and the author of *Eros the Bittersweet: An Essay* (Princeton, 1986) and *Short Talks* (Brick, 1992), as well as *Sophokles' Elektra* (a translation forthcoming from Oxford, 1994) and *Plainwater* (a collection of essays and verse forthcoming from Knopf, 1994). She is currently working for PBS television as writer and co-host of a documentary series called *The Nobel Legacy*, to be aired October 1994.

Richard Cumyn was born in Ottawa and educated at Queen's University at Kingston. He has published essays and articles in a number of Canadian newspapers and magazines, and his fiction has appeared in periodicals, including *The New Quarterly*, *The Canadian Forum*, and *NeWest*, as well as *The Grand-Slam Book of Canadian Baseball Writing*, an anthology (Pottersfield Press, 1993). "The Sound He Made" appears in his first and recent collection *The Limit of Delta Y Over Delta X* (Goose Lane Editions, 1994). Richard lives in Halifax and is at work on a second collection of stories.

Genni Gunn lives in Vancouver and writes in a variety of genres. Her publications include a novel, *Thrice Upon a Time* (Quarry Press, 1990), which was runner-up for Best First Book in the Canada/Caribbean region in the Commonwealth Prize; a short-story collection, *On the Road* (Oberon Press, 1991), whose title story was anthologized in *Best Canadian Stories 88*; a prose/poetry collection, *Mating in Captivity* (Quarry Press, 1993); and two translations from Italian of poetry collections by Dacia Maraini: *Devour Me Too* (Guernica Editions, 1987), finalist for the John Glassco Translation Award, and *Travelling in the Gait of a Fox* (Quarry Press, 1992). She has recently completed an original opera libretto, *Alternate Visions*, commissioned by Vancouver Opera, to be performed in the 1995-96 season. Her current projects include a screen-play adaptation of her novel *Thrice Upon a Time* under Telefilm Canada's Cross-Over Writers Program, and a new short-story collection.

Melissa Hardy was born and raised in Chapel Hill, North Caro-lina. From 1966 to the present day her father, novelist William Hardy, has worked for the Cherokee Historical Association. As a result she spent seven summers on the Qualla Boundary, the reservation of the Eastern Band of the Cherokee Nation in the mountains of western North Carolina, where "Long Man the River" and the story cycle of which it forms a part, *Constant Fire* (Oberon Press, forthcoming), is set. Melissa's first novel, *A Cry of Bees*, was published by Viking Press in 1970. Recently she has published in *Canadian Author and Bookman*, *Quarry*, *The Antigonish Review*, *The Dalhousie Review*, *Exile*, and *The New Quarterly*. She lives in London, Ontario, and is presently working on a second story cycle about the Cherokee entitled *Dreamcatcher*.

Robert Mullen lives in Edinburgh, Scotland, where he pres-ently writes full time. "Anomie" will be appearing in a collec-tion of his stories, *Towards the Light*, due out this fall from Coteau Books.

Vivian Payne grew up in Northern Ontario and is presently teaching in downtown Toronto. Some of her stories have been published in *A Room of One's Own* magazine, and one of her plays, *Celery*, was produced by Alumnae Theatre. She is the originator of *First Draft*, a monthly reading series promoting new Canadian playwrights. She is working on more stories and a full-length stage play about her home town, North Bay.

Jim Reil was born in Victoria, where he studied writing with W.D. Valgardson, Jack Hodgins, and Audrey Thomas. He now lives near Ottawa and works as a freelance writer. "Dry" is his first published story.

Robyn Sarah was born in 1949 and has lived in Montreal for most of her life. She has published five poetry collections, most recently *The Touchstone* (Anansi, 1992), and one collection of short stories, *A Nice Gazebo* (Vehicule Press, 1992). She is at work on new poems, and has a second story collection nearing completion.

Joan Skogan has spent most of her life living and working on the west coast of British Columbia. She has an MA in Creative Writing from the University of Victoria and has published several children's books, including *Grey Cat at Sea* and *The Princess and the Sea-Bear*, and an adult book, *Skeena, the River Remembered*. Her most recent publication is a work of adult non-fiction about her adventures at sea as a fisheries observer on foreign fishing trawlers called *Voyages: At Sea with Strangers*. She is currently living on Gabriola Island in British Columbia.

Dorothy Speak was born in Seaforth, Ontario, and grew up in nearby Woodstock. She attended McMaster and Carleton Universities and has lived in Ottawa for the past seventeen years. Her stories have been published widely in Canadian and American literary journals. Her first short-story collection, *The Counsel of the Moon*, was published in 1990 (Random House). She has completed a second story collection and has now embarked on a novel.

Alison Wearing began travelling at the age of seventeen and currently resides at no fixed address. Travel and political commentary have appeared in the *Globe and Mail* and *Queen's Quarterly*. "Notes from Under Water" is her first piece of published fiction. She is currently at work on *Solitary Motion*, a collection of travel stories told through the voice of a woman travelling alone.

About the Contributing Journals

Descant is a quarterly literary magazine which publishes poetry, prose, fiction, interviews, travel pieces, letters, photographs, engravings, art, and literary criticism. Editor: Karen Mulhallen. Managing Editor: Elizabeth Mitchell. Submissions and correspondence: P.O. Box 314, Station P, Toronto, Ontario, M5S 2S8.

Event is published three times a year by Douglas College, in New Westminster, B.C. It focusses on fiction, poetry, and reviews by new and established writers, and every spring it runs a Creative Non-Fiction contest. Now in its twenty-third year of publication, *Event* has won national awards for its writers. Editor: Dale Zieroth. Fiction Editor: Maurice Hodgson. Submissions and correspondence: P.O. Box 2503, New Westminster, B.C., V3L 5B2.

Exile is a quarterly that features Canadian fiction and poetry as well as the work of writers in translation from all over the world; some the best-known, others unknown. Publisher and Editor: Barry Callaghan. Submissions and correspondence: Box 67, Station B, Toronto, Ontario, M5T 2C0.

The Malahat Review publishes mostly fiction and poetry and includes a substantial review article in each issue. We are open to dramatic works, so long as they lend themselves to the page; we welcome literary works that defy easy generic categorization. Editor: Derk Wynand. Associate Editor: Marlene Cookshaw. Assistant Editor: Lucy Bashford. Submissions and correspondence: University of Victoria, P.O. Box 1700, MS 8524, Victoria, B.C., V8W 2Y2.

NeWest is a bi-monthly magazine that covers the cultural, social, and political scene in Western Canada in a variety of genres – feature articles, short essays, interviews, and reviews. In addition, *NeWest* features the poetry and fiction of writers – new or established – from across Canada. We publish up to ten stories a year, including an annual fiction issue. The magazine was founded in Edmonton in 1975 and has been based in Saskatoon since 1983. Editorial Committee: Paul Denham, Dave Glaze, John Lavery, William Robertson, Gail Youngberg. Fiction Editor: William Bartley. Submissions and correspondence: P.O. Box 394, RPO University, Saskatoon, Saskatchewan, S7N 9Z9.

The New Quarterly promotes new writers and new kinds of writing with a special interest in work which stretches the bounds of realism. We publish poetry, short fiction, essays on writing, and interviews with occasional special issues on themes and genres in Canadian writing. Submissions and correspondence: c/o ELPP, PAS 2082, University of Waterloo, Waterloo, Ontario, N2L 3G1.

Prairie Fire is a quarterly magazine of contemporary Canadian writing which regularly publishes stories, poems, book reviews, and visual art by emerging as well as established writers and artists. *Prairie Fire*'s editorial mix also occasionally features critical and personal essays, interviews with authors, and readers' letters. *Prairie Fire* commissions an illustration for each story and every summer publishes a fiction issue. Some of *Prairie Fire*'s most popular issues have been double-sized editions on multicultural themes, individual authors, and different genres. *Prairie Fire* publishes writing from, and has readers in, virtually all parts of Canada. Editor: Andris Taskans. Fiction Editors: Heidi Harms, Susan Rempel Letkemann, and Joan Thomas. Submissions and correspondence: Rm. 423 – 100 Arthur St., Winnipeg, Manitoba, R3B 1H3.

For more than thirty years, **Prism international** has published work by writers both new and established, Canadian and international. Edited by graduate students of creative writing at the University of British Columbia, *Prism* looks for innovative fiction, poetry, drama, as well as creative non-fiction, in English or English translation. *Prism* also holds an annual fiction contest. Request guidelines or send submissions to: The Editors, *Prism international*, Department of Creative Writing, BUCH E462 – 1866 Main Mall, University of British Columbia, Vancouver, B.C., V6T 1Z1.

Founded in 1893, **Queen's Quarterly** is the oldest intellectual journal in Canada. It publishes articles on a variety of subjects and consequently fiction occupies relatively little space. There are one or two stories in each issue. However, because of its lively format and eclectic mix of subject matter, *Queen's Quarterly* attracts readers with widely diverse interests. This exposure is an advantage many of our fiction writers appreciate. Submissions are welcome from both new and established writers. Fiction Editor: Joan Harcourt. Submissions and correspondence: Queen's University, Kingston, Ontario, K7L 3N6.

The Journey Prize Anthology
List of Previous Contributors

1
1989

Ven Begamudré, "Word Games"
David Bergen, "Where You're From"
Lois Braun, "The Pumpkin-Eaters"
Constance Buchanan, "Man With Flying Genitals"
Ann Copeland, "Obedience"
Marion Douglas, "Flags"
Frances Itani, "An Evening in the Café"
Diane Keating, "The Crying Out"
Thomas King, "One Good Story, That One"
Holley Rubinsky, "Rapid Transits" *
Jean Rysstad, "Winter Baby"
Kevin Van Tighem, "Whoopers"
M. G. Vassanji, "In The Quiet of a Sunday Afternoon"
Bronwen Wallace, "Chicken 'N' Ribs"
Armin Wiebe, "Mouse Lake"
Budge Wilson, "Waiting"

2
1990

André Alexis, "Despair: Five Stories of Ottawa"
Glen Allen, "The Hua Guofeng Memorial Warehouse"
Marusia Bociurkiw, "Mama, Donya"
Virgil Burnett, "Billfrith the Dreamer"
Margaret Dyment, "Sacred Trust"
Cynthia Flood, "My Father Took a Cake to France" *
Douglas Glover, "Story Carved in Stone"
Terry Griggs, "Man With the Axe"
Rick Hillis, "Limbo River"
Thomas King, "The Dog I Wish I Had, I Would Call it Helen"

5
1993